Edwina Shaw is a an
emerging Australian writer
with several short stories
published in journals and
collections. Two of her pieces
were shortlisted for Australia's
prestigious Josephine Ulrick
Literature Prize. She is also an
experienced teacher and holds a
BA in English and a Masters in
Creative Writing.

She has taught maths to
young offenders, English to
migrants and refugees, opened a
private English language school
in Cambodia, and now teaches
yoga and creative writing to
adults and high school children.
Thrill Seekers is dedicated
to the memory of her brother
Matthew, who developed
schizophrenia and committed
suicide at the age of twenty. It
is her first full-length novel.

IN THE SAME SERIES

A Forgotten Tomorrow
TERESA SCHAEFFER

Breaking Dawn
DONNA SHELTON

Bone Song
SHERRYL CLARK

Don't Even Think It
HELEN ORME

Ecstasy
A. C. FLANAGAN

Gun Dog
PETER LANCETT

Hanging in the Mist
PETER LANCETT

Marty's Diary
FRANCES CROSS

MindF**k
FANIE VILJOEN

Scarred Lions
FANIE VILJOEN

Seeing Red
PETER LANCETT

See You on the Backlot
THOMAS NEALEIGH

Stained
JOANNE HICHENS

The Finer Points of Becoming Machine
EMILY ANDREWS

The Only Brother
CAIAS WARD

The Questions Within
TERESA SCHAEFFER

Thrill Seekers

EDWINA SHAW

Thrill Seekers

EDWINA SHAW

Series Editor: Peter Lancett

Published by Ransom Publishing Ltd.
Radley House, 8 St. Cross Road, Winchester, Hampshire, SO23 9HX, UK
www.ransom.co.uk

ISBN 978 184167 8801

First published in 2011
Copyright © 2011 Ransom Publishing Ltd.
Front cover photograph: © Betsy Dupuis

In loving memory of my brother Matthew

1967 – 1987

and for all the boys.

Acknowledgements

I would like to thank the many people whose contributions have made this book possible. Peter Lancett, who saved Thrill Seekers from the scrap heap and helped bring it to its current form, and to Nigel and Jenny at Ransom for not giving up. Helena Pastor and Marion Howes, who know this book almost as well as I do, for their tireless editing, support and friendship. Katherine Howell, Favel Parrett and all my MPHIL and Joondo 8 friends for being a great cheering squad and sympathetic listeners. Veny Armanno, Amanda Lohrey, the late Jan McKemmish, Ben Ball and Barbara Mobbs for their advice and encouragement. My landlords, Romeo and Josephine Ercole, patrons of the arts, whose generosity and cheap rent has enabled me to stay at home and write. My husband Matthias and our children Bonnie and Tom, who gave me the time, space and love that I needed. My old friends, Steven, Marina, Patrick, Kay, Claire, Ivan, Suzi, Lulu and Paul; and my mother Natalie and siblings Natasha, Liam and Paula, who know the truth.

CHAPTER 1

Three Days

Brian

Look. See that box? My dad's in there, in that box they're putting into the ground.

I can hear him scratching on the lid.

I want to scream and jump in after the clump of dirt they get me to throw, pull off the lid and rescue him. But my legs won't move and I stand like an empty tin man as the mud thuds on top of the shiny wood, muffling the sound of his fingernails tearing.

Two weeks ago Dad told us he was dying. Me and my little brother Douggie sitting there eating breakfast like it was any other day, Vegemite toast turning hard in my throat. Mum sucking the guts out of a cigarette and blowing it out towards the window, not looking at us.

'I'm not going to get better,' he said.

'Oh,' we said. 'Oh.'

What did he mean, I wondered. He'd been sick a long time, become skinny and bald and ugly, but people always got better. You got sick, you took your medicine no matter how bad it tasted, and then you were better. That's how it went.

'I'm going to die,' he said, then got up and left us sitting there.

'Mum?' I said. 'It's not true, is it?'

Douggie didn't say anything, just sat there with a half-chewed piece of Weetbix still in his open mouth, his eyes big and wide like a possum's in torchlight.

'Mum? He's joking right?'

Mum blew out the last of her smoke and ground the butt into her ashtray. 'Of course he's not joking, Brian,' she sighed. 'Your father's sick. Maybe you'd have realised if you weren't always off playing the fool with your friends on that bloody creek. Don't you notice anything that's going on around here? He's very sick. He's going to die.'

'I don't get it.'

'What's there to get? You're big enough to understand, to start pulling your weight around here.' She rubbed her forehead. 'You're going to have to be the man of the house soon. I can't do it on my own. I just can't.'

'You mean he's really going to die?'

'For God's sake, how plain do I have to make it?' She gulped the last of her tea. 'Yes. He's going to die. D.I.E.'

'You mean like Fluffy?' Douggie got it quicker than me. Our guinea pig had been mauled by the neighbour's red setter last winter and we'd had to bury the bits in a shoebox under the Poinciana tree.

'Like Fluffy.' Mum nodded to Douggie with a closed-lip smile.

He started to cry, even though he's only about a year younger than me, and Mum held him close and patted his hair.

'Sorry,' she said. 'I'm sorry boys. I don't know what we're going to do.' She glanced over like she expected me to cry too.

I didn't. I'm thirteen, way too big to cry. Anyway I didn't feel like crying. I was trying to figure it all out. It couldn't really be true. Guinea pigs, cats, dogs, people on TV, soldiers, they die. Not ordinary people like us. The nuns reckon Jesus died then came back to life again three days later. Old people, they die. Dads don't.

I couldn't eat anymore, it all tasted like the box we'd buried Fluffy in. I left Mum and Douggie holding on to each other at the table and went to my room, closed the door and lay on top of my unmade bed listening to the washing machine go round and round and round.

When I couldn't stand the whirring any longer, I got down on my knees and pointed my fingers to heaven like the nuns had taught me and promised to be good forever if only God would change His mind. I promised I'd never tease Douggie again, or pull his hair or make fun of the stupid way he talks. I'd make my bed and help Mum wash up and never talk back or sneak any more ciggies or money from her purse. I'd do all my homework and not throw rocks from the overpass. I wouldn't even think about touching girls' tits. I'd grow up and be a priest. I'd do that and never have any fun ever again, if that would make God change His mind. I made a deal, a bargain to save Dad's life. It felt like God was listening.

I made my bed straight away, tucked in the corners and folded down the sheet. I put on my school uniform and rubbed the mud off my sneakers with a bit of toilet paper wet with spit, gathered up the clothes from the floor and chucked them in the laundry. God was watching. I wasn't going to let Dad down.

'Come on Douggie, stop crying,' I said as I dragged him down the path to school. 'It's going to be all right. I've fixed everything.'

My teacher, Sister Bernadette, kept looking at me funny. She must have thought I was about to put pins on her chair again, because she couldn't seem to understand why I was being so good all of a sudden. At the end of the week she made me wear the best student Holy Medal home. That made Dad smile. But it didn't make him better.

He stopped going to work, which wasn't like Dad, and lay in bed all day coughing, with Mum and Gran and strange nurses fussing over him. When I tried to get him to laugh or play with the ball they said 'Hush' and 'Leave your father in peace'. So I took Douggie out to the backyard instead and we kicked the football to each other in silence. It wasn't fun anymore. It seemed like nothing was fun.

Every night I prayed hard, made more promises, told God I'd get Douggie to be a priest too if that would help. But as the days wore on and Dad got thinner and greyer and the stink in his room started to turn me away, I knew that God wasn't listening. Had never been listening. And that even Mother Mary in her long blue gown didn't see me, there on my knees, by my bed, crying.

The deal was off. I stole half a packet of Mum's Marlboros and headed down to the creek with my mates. Smoked up a storm.

The sun kept shining like always. I went to school every day and pretended I was normal. But it felt like I wasn't really me at all. The real me who used to laugh and tease and chase after the girls had disappeared, gone away camping. He'd left me, some sort of robot double, to keep on doing the stupid things I had to do every day.

It wasn't me.

On the day before Dad died I went in and sat beside him on the bed, trying not to look at the way his skull showed through the skin on his face and his bald head, the way the tube sticking out of his arm bulged up the skin. Tried to see Dad the way he used to be, before cancer turned him into something scary.

'Hey,' he said. His lips were cracked, white pasty stuff was sticking in the corners, and his breath smelled bad.

'Dad, I…um…' The words wouldn't come. I wanted to say, 'Please don't die. Don't go and leave me behind.' But I couldn't.

'Brian, listen to me.' He coughed and scrunched up his face. I handed him a tissue from the box on the bedside table that was crammed with pill bottles and a vase of flowers with brown edges and dirty water. 'You take care of your mother and your brother for me. Okay?'

I nodded.

'Be a good boy.' He coughed again and lay back on his pillows with his eyes closed, holding onto his belly.

'I will.'

He didn't say any more, just lay there breathing hard and raspy, a deep crease between his eyebrows.

'I love you Dad,' I whispered as I rested my head to his bony chest. I lifted his arm and put it, loose and floppy, around my shoulders. But I couldn't stay there long because of the stink that was coming from under the sheets. It smelt like the dump where we go hunting for treasures. Something rotten.

Mum came in and bustled me out. She didn't like us kids being in there bothering Dad. She looked almost as skinny as him and was smoking more than ever. I'd even seen her helping him to have a drag on her cigarette, putting the butt up to his crusted lips, brushing them with her fingertips, smoothing back where his hair should have been with her other hand.

The day he died they sent us to school like it was any other day. Pushed us into the bedroom and told us to kiss Dad goodbye. He was still sleeping. I bent down to kiss him on the lips. But they were so awful, so death-ugly, that I changed my mind and gave him a quick kiss on the forehead. I should've kissed him on the lips. I would have, if I'd known that goodbye was forever.

And so, sometime around lunchtime on Thursday, while I picked at a peanut paste sandwich and pretended to smile at some kid's stupid joke in the school yard, Dad died. Later, one of my aunties came and picked me up early from school. I knew as soon as I heard the school gate clanking that it had happened. I tried not to see Aunty Joan, willed it not to be her, even tried praying again, but she got nearer and nearer until she stood at the classroom door with her eyes swollen, twisting a man's hanky in her hands. She whispered to Sister in the doorway, dark evil figures against the afternoon sun. Sister kept glancing over at me with a frown, nodding and frowning some more.

Her sensible nun shoes tapped to the front of the classroom.

'Class,' she said. 'I have some bad news. Brian's father has died. He has to go home.'

I wanted to smash her wrinkly old nun face into the floorboards. She told. I hadn't told anyone, not even my best mate, Jacko. On purpose. I didn't want any of them to know. Not until I was ready. Till I'd figured it out. Till I could joke about it so they wouldn't look at me like I was some kind of freak, which is what they were doing now, their eyes and mouths gaping.

Aunty Joan came over and wrapped her arm around me. I shrugged it off, gathered my stuff and walked out without looking at anyone. I could never go back in there again.

That afternoon the sky turned black just like the bible said it did the day Jesus died. It cracked open with thunder and heavy rain and I stood in the middle of our street until my clothes were soaked, letting the rain hide my tears. Trying to feel real. To get clean again. But I couldn't clean my insides.

The house was full of aunties and uncles, all talking. There were cakes and biscuits, even some with chocolate, but I wasn't hungry. I didn't want treats. I wanted Dad back. And if I couldn't have that I wanted the house quiet, just me and Mum and Douggie, so I could think. So we could make a circle together and understand that our number had gone from four to three.

But Mum was surrounded by an army of grown ups who wouldn't let me near her, who kept pouring booze that smelt like Christmas pudding into her glass, lighting her cigarettes, telling me to shush and let my mother be. No one even noticed I was wet.

I couldn't see Douggie anywhere. Then I glimpsed him hiding under the kitchen table, curled into a ball sucking his thumb. Mum had made him stop doing that ages ago. I got down on my hands and knees on the lino and crawled between the wall of stockinged legs to join him. When I got close I heard him making a funny whimpering sound, like a dog that's been locked out.

'Douggie,' I whispered. 'Doug?'

He didn't take the thumb out of his mouth, but he looked at me. He looked so scared that it made me feel brave and I put my hand on his back and patted him a bit.

He uncurled then and came to me, tried to bury himself in my puny wet chest.

I'm going to have to look after him. But I don't know how.

Douggie's not here today. They said he was too upset to come, too young. Not me though. I'm thirteen. Old enough for a funeral. Old enough to look after everyone. Douggie, and Mum too.

So I can't jump in after Dad, no matter how much I want to.

Anyway, you never know what might happen. Remember Jesus? He died, but He wasn't really dead. So I'll wait.

I'll wait three days.

I waited three days; I've waited three bloody years. God sucks.

CHAPTER 2
Voices

Brian

I hear them talking in the dark. I hear Douggie sobbing, telling Mum everything, things mothers aren't supposed to know. And I'm angry with him for being so weak. Angry with him for breaking the rules, for telling and getting us all into trouble.

We've been at the local park together, the Oxley Creek boys, wearing footy jerseys and jeans against the cold of a Brisbane winter night. My little brother Douggie, his best mate Steve, Russ from down the road, Jacko and me, have been drinking all day, the usual casks of moselle. It's Saturday so we've had time on our hands. No bloody school. Some of the others dribbled in after footy and work at the garage and tried to catch up. Jacko drove his heap of shit bomb to the pub and bought spirits – bottles of vodka and rum and scotch, and litres of coke to mix with it. It was going to be a big night. No special reason, just Saturday.

We scored an ounce of dope from school yesterday and there's still most of it left, despite us smoking a dent in it last night, bonging on in the cubby-house down the back of our place. It's on the banks of the creek, camouflaged by mangroves and overgrown bamboo, an old chook shed we've fixed up and turned into the best cubby in the street. We've got cushions and carpet, and even electricity to plug in the CD player and the heater on cold nights – the perfect place for endless weekend sessions.

But tonight the party got too big for the cubby. Fellas we didn't even know that well turned up hoping for a smoke, waving bottles of rum and pretending we were best mates. It was getting way too crowded and noisy and Mum was freaking, so we moved to the park.

We scrambled under the barbed wire fence at the end of the street, cut through the paddock and spooked the skittish white horse that lived there. It chased after Douggie, almost biting him on the arse, and we all cracked up. As we crossed the field to the park, streetlights lit up the fog floating in the gullies, like smoke machine effects in a rock video. We sat on benches in the black shadow of fig trees near the creek and partied on.

It was a dark night, no moon, and finger-burning cold. The booze warmed us but not enough, so we made a bonfire, first with fallen branches and rubbish from bins, then with the bench we were sitting on. It was heavy, weighted down with cement blocks buried in the earth, but with all of us rocking it forward and back, heaving and falling, we managed to drag it onto the flames. Sparks flew up into the sky, spraying high firework orange against the night.

We laughed, and sang stupid songs, boasted about girls we'd had, played air guitar, and clapped sticks together. We pretended we were Abos and danced around the fire, swivelling our feet on the slippery grass, acting like crazy birds and hunters. The dope made us laugh. Well, usually it did. But we weren't laughing much tonight. A bad mood hung in the air, hovering over each of us, but mainly over Douggie.

I've noticed it happening to him over the last few weeks, especially when we've been smoking the really strong heads. He hasn't been able to keep up. His eyes get that stupid glazed-over half-crossed look and he starts speaking bullshit. Hearing stuff that no one says, getting paranoid. We all noticed.

Even so, Steve couldn't understand it when suddenly Douggie said, 'Fucken shut up, Steve. I know what you've been saying about me. What you've been doing, you bastard!'

'I haven't been doing nothing. What're you on about?'

I was sitting between them, my arse cold and wet on the dewy grass, my face roasting in the fire. Steve hadn't said anything about Douggie.

'Don't bloody lie to me. I can hear you.'

Really, Steve hadn't said a thing.

'Keep your shirt on, Doug. You're my best mate. Why would I say something?'

'I don't know. I don't know.' Douggie shook his head, then started getting all teary, choking up. Everyone else had gone quiet. The screech of fruit bats echoed in the dark.

'Fuck you, you arsehole!' Douggie yelled. 'Don't pretend. Don't lie to me!'

He leapt up and started laying into Steve, his small fists hard and pointy. Steve's much bigger than Douggie, all rugby player, no neck, and he didn't want to fight. They've been best mates since grade three. But Douggie was hurting him, drawing blood. So he struck back. Holding onto each other they punched at close range, fight-dancing too close to the fire. The fellas we didn't know made a circle and started the chant.

'Fight, fight, fight.'

'Douggie! Stop it!' I yelled. 'He didn't say anything.'

I tried to pull them apart but only got whacked for my efforts, punched from both sides. Jacko and Russ came running to give me a hand. We were mates, blood-brothers, the Oxley Creek boys. We fought other people, not each other. Russ held Steve back while Jacko grabbed Douggie's arms and helped me pull him off. He was throwing wild punches and swearing, his face distorted and ugly in the firelight, saliva and blood spraying as he screamed.

'You bastard! You fucken bastard! You're supposed to be my friend. How could you do that to me? How could you say that?'

'Shit Douggie, I haven't said anything. You're crazy, bloody crazy!'

'Fuck youse!' roared Douggie and wrestled free of our arms, wriggling out of his jersey, leaving us holding only its emptiness, the shell of the boy that once was. He ran off into the foggy night, running from the demons that were chasing him.

He's my little brother but I didn't run after him. I sat there with the others, consoling Steve, drinking more, rolling another joint, shaking my head over Douggie losing it. I stayed on with our mates while he ran off into the darkness alone. Because I was afraid. I was afraid of the voices he heard that were so real to him, afraid that if I listened hard enough I'd hear them too. And if I heard them then everyone would be shaking their heads over me, and calling me a 'fucken mad bastard' too.

The fire died down and everyone but our gang went home. We didn't have the strength left to move another bench, so we pissed on the embers till they were soaked and headed back to the cubby. We went back the secret way, scrambling along the creek-bank, sliding and falling into the mud.

Back at home I went to get some water from the laundry under the house. It was late, after three, Mum was asleep for sure. With any luck Douggie would've found his way to bed to sleep it off. There was no Dad to wake up. No Dad to come waving his belt as a threat, roaring at me about looking after my brother. Maybe Douggie would've been able to keep it together if Dad was still around. He was always Dad's favourite. Douggie's never been the same since Dad died. He's too soft. It doesn't pay to be soft. It's different for me. I'm older. I'm hard.

I'm at the back of the house, the unmown grass wetting my jeans, when I hear them.

The voices. I hear Douggie crying, telling Mum everything, about the fight and the drugs and the booze. Then I hear Mum, but it doesn't sound like her. She isn't yelling. She doesn't even sound angry. Her voice is soft and low, coming from Douggie's room, a gentle rumble, comforting him, telling him that everything's going to be all right – that he's going to be all right.

And I'm angry. Angry with Douggie for being so weak, for running and telling, for dobbing and getting us all into trouble. I'm angry and guilty and sad. A groan escapes the back of my throat. He's my little brother and I didn't even stand by him. I should've stopped him smoking when he first started hearing shit. I should've taken the bong away, stopped him drinking, listened and tried to understand. But I didn't do anything.

I stand cemented to the grass, listening and hating myself. The sound of Douggie's pathetic whimpers, and my mother comforting him, cuts me deeper than I can bear.

Forcing my legs to move I take the three extra steps to the laundry and pick up one of Mum's empty vodka bottles from the floor. I turn on the cold tap over the grimy cement tub, but it squeals and sings in its rusty pipes. I turn it off in a hurry but it's too late. There's quiet, then...

'Brian?' Mum calls. 'Brian is that you? Come here, love.'

I don't answer. I have no voice.

I drop the bottle, smashing it into the tub, and run, my heart thumping, back down the hill to the cubby. Almost there I retch and heave, vomiting violently, black-red like old blood. I wipe my mouth and my eyes on my jersey and go back in to the fellas.

Everyone's asleep but Steve. He's holding the bong close to his battered lips and crying.

'Shut up,' I say and snatch the bong away.

I grab the whisky and drain the last of it in a couple of burning swigs. I pack and pull three huge cones in a row, till I can't feel the ache in my guts anymore.

I'm sixteen. Douggie's fifteen.

He isn't all right. He'll never be all right again.

CHAPTER 3

Douggie and the Paparazzi

Douggie

I'm better looking than Justin Timberlake. And a better dancer. He knows it too. Jealous as hell. They all are. You can't be this good looking and not put a few noses out of joint.

Ever noticed how much your face changes? It does. I've been watching mine in the mirror. My nose is getting longer every day. I hope it doesn't get too big and ruin my career. My cheekbones are lifting too. Sometimes they move up while I'm watching. It's a bit freaky really, but I'm used to it now. You'd probably notice yours moving too, if you looked for long enough.

I love taking off all my clothes and wanking in front of the mirror. Watching myself come. I'm so fucking hot. Just ask any of the girls in the hospital, they can't get enough of me. Even the nurses. They're all after a piece of my perfect arse and huge banana dick. I had some pretty good times in there. You've gotta make the best of a bad situation. Still, I won't be going back in a hurry.

The price of fame is getting pretty bloody high. If they're not after your body, they're burning up with jealousy and plotting against you. It's not easy to stay positive.

They've stashed all the money from my modelling assignments and films in some Swiss bank account, so I'm stuck trying to survive, buy clothes and makeup and stuff, on Mum's measly pocket money.

Then there's the Paparazzi, always snapping me when I least expect it. Like before, when I was in the shower. Someone sneaked in and took photos of me through the glass, nude. That's the shot they all want. My gorgeous arse plastered across the front page would sell a lot of papers. But still, if they want to photograph me naked they should at least ask first. I'd come up much better with proper lighting and some oil and a workout beforehand. But no, they've got to do it on the sly, creep around and snap me when I'm not looking my best, so they don't have to pay. I'm owed millions.

I don't know how they get into the house. Mum and Brian must be in on it. Trying to make some extra money from my fame. They probably take a cut of the fee and let the bastards in. I can't trust anyone round here. They're nice as pie to my face but the moment my back is turned they're whispering against me, scheming and plotting ways to take me down, steal my money. And I love these people. I'd never do anything like that to them. Is money enough to betray your own flesh and blood? I try not to think about it. Stay positive. I don't know why they do it, but it hurts.

'Doug, are you almost finished in there? I've got to go.' That's Mum. She doesn't like it when I'm in here too long.

'I'm shaving.'

'Oh, all right then. Just hurry would you?' Then something else I can't quite make out, something about body or bloody and money.

That'd be right, she's probably organising stuff with the Paparazzi right now. I wrap a towel around my waist. They're going to have to pay if they want a photo of the best cock on the planet.

'Where were you last night?' she asks through the door.

'Out.' She's trying to trace my movements. Is it only for the Paparazzi? Maybe she's got something to do with my Swiss bank.

'I knew that. Where did you go?'

'None of your business.' I was out partying, picking up girls, showing them all a few new moves. But I wasn't going to tell Mum that.

'I was very worried, you know. You shouldn't be going out at all. Remember what the doctor said.'

'Why not?' See, what did I tell you? It's like being under house arrest. Fame. I'm glad I'm a star and that, but it sure has some serious drawbacks. Like a forty-year old woman telling me what I can and can't do.

'I was going to call the police.'

That'd be right. Anything to get me out of the way. Locked up.

'Doug?' I don't answer, so she stomps away.

I splash the shaving cream off my face, put on my eyeliner, and start getting dressed. I'm putting on the new silk shirt I nicked when I hear them. Men's voices. The Paparazzi. Or is it? They've got some sort of accent. Swiss?

I bust open the door. But there's no one there, just Mum in the kitchen stacking the dishwasher. She jumps at the bang of the door, looks up like I've caught her doing something wrong.

Was it her? It sounded like men but it could've been Mum disguising her voice.

'About time,' she says, heading for the toilet.

'Where are they?'

'Who?'

'Don't play the innocent with me. I know someone's here.'

'There's no one here. You must be hearing voices again. Did you take your pills this morning?' She comes over with her hand stretched out to my forehead like she's going to take my temperature.

'Don't try that shit with me,' I say knocking her hand away. 'Where are they?'

'Oh Douggie,' she sighs, turning. 'Anyway, I've got to go to the toilet. What do you do in there for so long anyway?'

I give her a dirty look. She can roll her eyes and play dumb all she wants. I know what she's up to, and it isn't good. I know there was someone here. I heard them. I'm not an idiot. I know what's going on. They think I'm crazy but I know what's real and what's not, what I see and hear. I don't believe in God anymore because I can't hear or see Him, but I sure as hell can hear these bastards plotting against me. I rush down the hallway to my room and slam the door shut. I wish there was someone I could trust. I wish Dad was here.

But I'm not going to let the bastards get to me. Not today. Got to stay focused, stay positive. I had a great night and I'm going to have a good weekend. I scored last night so I'm going to smoke a joint and be normal, like in the old days, write some songs and learn a few more chords on my guitar.

I sit down on my bed and roll a two-paper joint. Perfect. My brother Brian's always up for a smoke. I'll give him a ring over at Jacko's and see if they want to meet me in the cubby for a session. It hasn't been the same around here lately. Brian's always over at Jacko's, practically lives there though he's still got his room here next to mine. Some nights he comes home for dinner. Most of the time it's just me and the old lady rattling around.

I go out to the lounge to dial his number. Mum is watching some romance DVD, a tumbler of vodka in one hand and a cigarette in the other.

'What are you doing?' she asks over her shoulder.

'Ringing Brian if that's okay with you, or do I have to ask permission to ring my own brother these days?'

She grunts and turns back to the TV.

It's been a while since I've seen Brian. Not since my sixteenth birthday a couple of months ago, just before they put me in hospital. I'd told him to get the old gang together for the party to end all parties. I was putting on a keg. I sold my bike to buy it. I made lots of cool party tapes, hung streamers, blew up balloons, got ready and waited.

No one came. Not one of the bastards. Not even Steve. Jealous. Can't hack the pace because I'm famous now and they're all nobodies. But I didn't let it get to me. I showed them. I sat in the decorated cubby and drank that whole keg by myself. Took a few days, but I did it. Brian came and had a couple, but he didn't stay long, said he was busy over at Jacko's. Mum kept coming down, trying to make me stop and come to bed, looking at me with a stupid pitying look in her eyes. I hate that look. It makes me angry.

Brian answers the phone.

'Gidday Brian.'

'Douggie, how's it hangin?'

'Good. Got out yesterday. Want to come round for a smoke?'

'What, a joint?'

'Yeah.'

'You know you're not supposed to smoke anymore.'

'Do you always do what you're told?'

'That's different.'

'Why?'

'I'm not crazy.'

'Don't say that.'

'Face facts, you're fucked in the head.'

'Who says?'

'You're sick, mate. How many times do I have to tell you? It's schizophrenia.'

'What would you know? You're the fucking crazy one. You're the one who can't stop drinking, even for a day.'

'I don't have time for this. There are people here.'

'I'll come over there then.'

'No. You can't.'

'Why not?'

'It's just not on, all right.'

'Why?'

'There are girls and stuff, no one you know.'

'Girls love me, can't get enough of me.'

'That's what I mean.'

'What?'

'All your bullshit.'

'Jealous are you?'

'Yeah right. Look, I've gotta go. How about I come see you tomorrow? We can watch the footy together.'

'Don't you want a joint with your own brother?'

'No, Douggie, I don't. I'm busy. I've got things to do.'

'Fuck you.'

'See you tomorrow then?'

I hang up. I'm not going to cry. I run back to my room and slam the door. Brian was a real mate once. Now he's just another enemy, telling lies, saying I'm crazy, trapping me. I'm not bloody crazy. It's them, all of them plotting against me. They're the crazy ones. Why doesn't anyone believe me? They can all just go fuck themselves.

Sometimes, if I let myself believe them, I feel like I could throw myself off a bridge or something. If I believe their bullshit then I know what's ahead. I'm not stupid. I'll end up like the old guys in hospital, the ones who live on the streets between visits. I'll never get a job, no girl will ever want me, I'll never have kids – and I'd be a great dad too. There'd be nothing. So I can't believe them. I won't.

Still, sometimes it gets to me, and I give up. I've tried to top myself a couple of times, but it's harder to kill a body than you think. I jumped off the back verandah with the hose around my neck, but it stretched and I bounced halfway back up again, more bungee jump than noose. I tried leaping up and hitting my head into the ceiling fan to knock my brains out, but that didn't work either. I lay on the railway tracks and waited as a train approached, but then it rushed past on the other line, blowing train fart all over me.

When they start laying all the bloody crazy talk on me, telling me I'm a schizo, a fucking loon, it's enough to drive anyone to a bottle of pills. That's how I ended up in hospital this last time, after my birthday party. Pills.

I didn't take enough.

Anyway, that was before. I've got too much to live for now – my music, my movies, the fans, sex. I won't let the bastards get to me. I won't believe their lies. I'll show them all. There'll be a way through all this shit.

I'm going to sing a happy song.

CHAPTER 4
The Raft

Brian

Bloody Douggie. He's driving me totally fucking crazy. I mean, not mad-insane like him, just normal crazy. He's my little brother, and I love him, but it's not easy anymore. I wish I'd never let him join the Oxley Creek Boys. Wish he'd just stayed at home and read books or something girly like that. Then he'd be normal now, not a bloody loon I have to worry over, get sick to my guts about and find blue on the bathroom floor stuffed full of pills. I try to forget about it, you know, lead my own life and that, not let it get to me. But I can't help remembering him the way he used to be, the funny kid behind me in the dinghy, or on that stupid raft we made that best summer of all. The one before Dad died.

School was finished for the year, and only two days into the holidays we had the makings of a raft. The tin drums rolled like thunder down the street as we chased after them. They sounded like giants laughing, so happy they could bust. Like us. The sun scorched the back of our t-shirts and we all had sweat and dirt necklaces and black creases in our elbows as we tumbled the drums the rest of the way to the cubby.

Weeks earlier we'd found a huge old door at the dump and balanced it on our heads all the way home. We tried floating it by itself but ended up scrambling in mud up to our shorts trying to save the door from getting sucked under. Jacko said 'Told ya so,' but I swear it was his idea in the first place. He was fourteen then, and already the coolest kid around. He had that leather jacket his Dad gave him, which made him look like he could ride a Harley or something. He was the leader of our gang; still is really, though there's not much of a gang left anymore. I was the next boss, then Russ my mate from down the road, then Douggie and his friend Steve. The Oxley Creek Boys.

It was harder than we thought to put the drums and the door together in a way that worked. The ropes kept slipping and we didn't want to use nails in case it leaked. We smoked half a pack of ciggies trying to figure it out. It was my idea to nick some wire from the fence at the paddock to tie the barrels on. Dad came down with his drill to make the holes, four for each drum, so we could wrap the wire around and twist it tight to make them stable. We scrounged some more wire and did figure eights from one to the other so the barrels wouldn't pop out at the sides when we put the raft in the water. In the end it looked great, especially after we scabbed some paint out of the shed and wrote 'Thrill Seekers' on the top in red.

It took all five of us to drag the raft down over the mud to the water's edge. Half the kids in the neighbourhood had turned up to watch the launch. Beck, Russ's little sister, stood on the bank with the others, sniffling because she wanted to come too; but Jacko wouldn't let her. She was real cute in those days, red hair in piggy tails and all those freckles. Reckon I had a bit of a crush on her. But I wouldn't have said anything to Jacko to save my life. He hated girls. Funny how things turn out.

As we hauled the raft to the muddy bank I felt like I was some sort of a hero, or one of those native guys in Tarzan movies who went down the Amazon. We all held our breath as we slid the raft into the water. It floated! We danced like clowns on the bank and I tackled Jacko into the mud just for the hell of it.

'Unreal!' I yelled. 'Let's go.'

'Hang on, hang on,' said Jacko running back to the cubby, coming back waving a bottle in the air. 'Can't set off without christening it properly. It'd be bad luck. I've been saving this for something special, pinched it from the cupboard.'

He was holding a bottle of rum with a polar bear on the label, but there wasn't that much left, maybe a third.

'Here we go then,' he said, tapping it on the side of the raft near the writing. But the bottle didn't smash like it was supposed to.

'Use your muscles,' said Douggie. 'Go on, break it!'

'What and waste all this great booze?' Jacko said as he sat back up and unscrewed the cap, taking a big swig. Then he passed it to me.

It tasted pretty bad and burned like acid in my guts, but then I got that feeling that's all sort of golden. I love that feeling. I took another sip and let the feeling spread over my body. 'Great stuff,' I said and passed the bottle on to Russ. We shared it down the line till it was gone. We laughed and showed off, acting like the toughest kids ever.

Jacko smashed the empty bottle on the raft and chucked the end into the dirty brown creek yelling, 'Get on!' He bum-slid onto the raft and sat at the front, the captain's position. Warm with rum and sunshine, we clambered onboard, sitting so deep in the water that my undies were soaked. Russ and I were crammed next to each other behind Jacko, with Douggie and Steve behind us, their arses hanging off the back.

'Untie the rope, Douggie,' I yelled.

'Yeah,' said Jacko. 'Get the rope!'

Russ and I heaved the oars we'd made from orange crates and broomsticks into the water, dragging them backwards, feeling the pull of the creek. Our arms stung with the effort. But once we'd turned towards the dump it wasn't as hard as I thought it would be. Soon we were fairly racing along down the middle towards Pamphlet Bridge and the river.

'Yeehah!' I called out like in one of those old cowboy movies.

'Cool!' yelled Douggie, 'I wonder if this is how the explorers did it? Like us, just them and the boat and maybe wild Aborigines on the bank throwing spears.' He was like that in those days, always inventing some kind of crazy game.

'Unreal,' said Steve.

We all grinned like monkeys and laughed out loud. This was our best creek adventure ever. Beat mud-walking any day. We were right out in the middle, just us fellas, no Dad, no dinghy. Just us, on the raft we'd made with our own hands.

We were going pretty fast too. I thought I was an Olympic star rower. It was so easy, the mangroves just slipping by. As we rushed under the sewerage pipe down past Russ's place, the shade was only a second of coolness. In my head I saw myself on a podium, bending down for one of those gold medals.

'Can I have a turn at rowing?' begged Douggie from behind.

'No way,' I said. 'It'd be too hard for a kid like you.'

'Would not! Jacko, tell Brian to let me have a go.'

To my surprise Jacko said, 'Okay mate.' He must've been in a real good mood. 'Hand it over.'

'He won't be able to do it.'

'Just give the kid the oar. Give Steve a turn too.'

So Douggie and Steve got their turn and even with them rowing we were flying along.

'See,' said Douggie, rowing like a mad man, 'See how fast we're making it go?'

In no time we rounded the bend of the creek, where rusty washing machines and piles of old tyres and car doors from the dump were sliding down the banks into the mangroves, sinking into the mud. The dump's a long way from our house. We'd never been that far down the creek before.

'Maybe we'd better go back now,' I said. 'Dad always says not to go past the dump.'

'You're such a girl,' said Jacko.

'We don't have to if you don't want to,' I said, my face burning. 'That's okay. We can go right out onto the river.'

'Yeah!' squealed Douggie and Steve from the back, their arms turning like windmills. 'We'll row, let's do it.'

'I don't know if it's such a good idea,' said Russ, sounding like a full-on wimp.

'You wouldn't would you, you big sook,' says Jacko. 'I reckon it's a bloody good idea. It's a great raft. What's the problem?'

Russ shook his head a bit but didn't say anything.

Douggie and Steve shouted 'Yeah!' and rowed so fast their arms looked blurry.

Russ stared down at the water sloshing onto the raft but I didn't let him spoil my fun. We were used to him being sulky. Ever since his Mum and Dad split up, he was moody. Most of the time he was alright but just sometimes, you know. Not like me. Even then I knew we had to put all that sissy shit behind us, be strong like men and just have a good time. Sure would've liked another swig of that rum. Russ should've been like Jacko. Jacko's Dad beat the crap out of him all the time, but I never heard him complain or cry. If you're a boy you just don't, that's all there is to it.

The midday sun was beating down hard on my hair like a fire beanie and my stomach was starting to feel like I'd swallowed creek water. 'Maybe we should turn around, I'm not feeling too good.'

'Whatever.' Jacko shrugged. The back of his neck was burnt a brighter pink than Beck's favourite skirt.

'Aw!' Douggie and Steve groaned. I turned around to glare at them and saw that they weren't even rowing anymore; the oars were resting on their laps and their fingertips were trailing in the wash as we continued to speed towards the bridge.

'Hey, give us back the oars you two, you're not even doing anything. We've got to go home now.'

'No way.'

They picked up the oars and tried to back-paddle to turn us around. Water sprayed all over me so I used my hand to send a sheet of water back at them. We splashed at each other till we were soaked and laughing.

'Is anyone rowing this bloody thing?' asked Jacko, like he was a grown-up, bored with our games.

'Yeah, we are,' said Russ, grabbing the oar from Steve.

After a bit of a tussle I wrenched the other one back from Douggie. Then Russ and I tried to turn the raft.

It wasn't as easy as we thought. Rowing just on the right side tilted us too far and water sloshed over the door. So I back-paddled while Russ rowed on the right, full bore. We puffed for breath, our faces busting, arms quivering. Finally we were heading in the right direction, but even though we rowed as hard as we could, harder than we'd ever rowed the dinghy, we were still drifting backwards towards the bridge. And the river.

'Row!' yelled Jacko, like we weren't trying. 'Give me a bloody turn. You're all useless.' But even his fourteen year-old muscles didn't make any difference against the current. The raft was too heavy. Bloody door.

Douggie and Steve were pissing themselves laughing, like it was all a crazy joke. I jabbed Douggie hard with my elbow.

'Shut up!'

They covered their mouths but I still heard them smirking and giggling behind their hands.

Jacko gave his oar back to Russ. Counting together, we timed our strokes so that the oars went in at the same time, which worked better, but the water was pulling us backwards faster than we could drag ourselves forwards. The muscles in my arms were shuddering and my heart was beating out of my chest, but the best we could do was get the raft to stay still. Water churned up either side of the door, splashing onto us, but we weren't going anywhere.

'Bloody hell!' shouted Jacko. 'Can't you do anything? Give me another go.'

'We have to get over to the side,' I grunted as I passed my oar forward. 'Then we can pull ourselves along on the mangroves like when we get stuck mud-walking.'

'Since when are you the boss?' asked Jacko, but he started back-paddling so we turned around facing the bank.

That didn't make any difference either. We just floated down the creek sideways.

'We're going to get sucked into the river,' panted Russ. 'We'd better ditch the raft and swim for it.' I glanced sideways at him. He was splattered in mud, soaked with water, face red from busting a gut rowing; and he looked worried. He might have been right.

'No way!' yelled Jacko. 'There's no bloody way we're ditching this raft.'

I took Russ's oar and tried my hardest to work in time with Jacko so we moved in the right direction. Behind me I heard Douggie whispering to Steve, 'What if we go right out into the ocean and go all the way to Tahiti or Hawaii? That'd be so great.'

'We'll get hit by a barge or drown before that happens,' said Russ, shutting them up.

The bridge was in sight and getting closer fast, the river a wide churning sea behind it. If we were lucky we'd get close enough to a pylon to hang on till the tide changed.

'What's that?' asked Steve, squinting into the glare and pointing to the shade under the bridge.

Putting up my hand to cut down the glare I could just make out something. 'I see it... it's a boat. A speedboat.' As we got closer I saw the writing that was down one side. 'It's the police.'

'Wow,' said Douggie. 'Just like on telly.'

'Bloody pigs,' said Jacko, but I knew he was breathing a sigh of relief, just like me.

As we drifted closer, still paddling furiously to get to the bank, I saw a couple of heads popping up from the water near the boat. On the deck a policeman in a uniform with shiny badges spied us and yelled,

'What the hell are you boys doing out here? Go home!'

'We're trying,' shouted Russ. 'But we can't do it, the tide's too...' His voice cracked like he was about to cry.

'Don't sook out on us now,' I hissed at him.

'Pull over to the mangroves,' ordered the policeman.

We paddled hard as we could, but we still weren't getting anywhere.

'Jesus Christ! What sort of a fool raft have you got there?' yelled the cop, throwing us a rope. Jacko caught it on the full, like he did it all the time, rescuing a scrap of our pride.

'Thank God,' whispered Russ.

I rolled my eyes, but inside I was saying the same. Douggie was the only one who was disappointed that our trip into the river had been cancelled.

The policeman reeled us in and tied us to the back of his boat.

'That's the river, boys,' he said. 'You kids have got no business out there. What on earth did you think you were playing at?'

'Explorers,' Douggie called with a grin.

Jacko shouted over him, 'Nothing, we weren't doing nothing wrong.'

'Do your parents know you're out here all by yourselves?'

'Sure.' Jacko lied so easily.

'Hmph,' grunted the policeman. 'They should know better. The river's no place for kids. You fellas stay put till the tide changes. There's a serious dive going on here, police work. I don't want to be wasting time looking for you. Now, or ever.'

Then he left us alone and went back into the boat's cabin where we heard the static of the police radio.

Jacko laughed and pretended it was a great joke to be tied up to a police boat, and I reckoned it was pretty tough too. Something to show off about to the other kids in the street when we got back. Russ went quiet and sat staring at the spot where the divers came up every now and then.

'What do you reckon they're looking for?' he asked.

'A body, probably,' said Jacko, like it was nothing.

Then Douggie started singing the theme from that old TV show Gilligan's Island we watched on cable sometimes, which made us all laugh and sing along. We sang that one, then the Neighbours song, and the one from Home and Away, then Teenage Mutant Ninja Turtles, and some ads from TV, till we ran out of songs we all knew except for hymns, and that was way too daggy. So we talked about all the best motorbike stunts we'd ever seen, and how we were going to try them on our pushies. We talked about how we couldn't wait to be old enough to drive, how school sucked and how our footy team just had to play better next year. Till we couldn't think of anything else to say.

I felt like I hadn't eaten in days and I was so thirsty I would have drunk creek water if it wasn't salty and full of cholera, but still the policeman didn't let us go. The tide was really low, black mud covered in an oily slick of rainbow colours, stretching out on each side of the creek.

'We could swim in and mud-walk home,' Russ tried again. 'Come and get the raft back later.'

'Forget it,' said Jacko.

So we did, but I thought it was a good idea myself. It was boring sitting there and I was getting that hungry, I considered eating a catfish raw. I just wanted to be at home with a vegemite sandwich and an enormous cup of green cordial. Russ's head disappeared between his knees and Jacko was gritting his teeth, the way he always did when he was angry.

Douggie and Steve were lying on their bellies, paddling their bare legs in the water behind, dunking their hands and checking how long they could see their fingers before they disappeared in the brown. The water finally started flowing towards home again, sloshing back over the mud.

Then one of the divers came up and shouted something I couldn't quite make out. Something like, 'We've got her.' The guy on board got all excited and threw over a net attached to a pulley by a long rope. The diver in the water tugged off his mask and swiped at the red marks on his forehead, rubbed his eyes. He looked over at us and called out, 'Get those bloody kids out of here.' Then he wriggled his mask back on and dived under again.

We sat up and watched. 'They've found something,' whispered Jacko. The rope on the net stretched taut and the diver resurfaced. He waved to the policeman on the boat and yelled, 'Right to go.'

Jacko was practically jumping off the raft, he was that excited. 'We're going to see it fellas. We're going to see a real live body. Make that dead.' He laughed.

I didn't feel like laughing though. My guts were twisting right up to my throat. Russ's face had gone whiter than bread, and Douggie looked like he'd had his eyelids removed, his eyes were so wide.

The man on the boat started grinding on a winch. It looked like it was heavy.

I realised I was holding my breath and had to force myself to take in some new air.

'Get those kids away!' the diver yelled as he swam to the boat's ladder.

The other one bobbed up too. 'For God's sake Mal, what are you thinking? Let the boys go.'

'Might do them good,' he said. But he shrugged and stopped winching. He shouted at Jacko to untie the rope and reeled it in.

'Go straight back, you fellas. No mucking around. You hear? And tell your father he should have more sense. It could be one of you I'm bringing in. You got that! Get home!' He sounded angrier than he needed to be, we hadn't done anything wrong.

The divers scrambled onto the boat, flapping awkwardly in their flippers. They stood with their hands on their hips, watching me and Russ row around in clumsy circles until we finally got the raft pointing in the direction of home. Then they retreated to the cabin.

Once we were going straight, rowing was easy. Looking behind over my shoulder, I saw the man with the badges working hard, winding fast. I saw the top of the net rising from the water. It looked empty.

'There's nothing in it after all,' said Jacko, disappointed.

But it wasn't empty, it's just that what was in it wasn't very big. The net lifted out of the water like a deflated balloon. In the bottom there was a small shape, black and pinky-blue, curled in the muddy ropes that held it. A small arm, no bigger than Beck's, fell through a gap and hung down towards the water. As if it was waving us goodbye.

Once we'd rounded the bend Jacko made jokes about the police and how stupid they were, and boasted about how great and cool it was to have seen a body. How it made us heaps tougher than anyone. But to tell you the truth, I was never so happy to see my backyard and the cubby smiling at us from the bank. After dragging the raft up through the mud onto the grass, we lay panting and dirty beside it. Douggie rested his head on my belly and I was too buggered to shove him off.

I propped myself up on my elbows and stared at the murky brown ripples of the creek rushing in with the tide. It flooded over the mud and lapped at the mangroves, washing away the oil slicks and covering the black. The current sure was strong. Soon I couldn't see any mud at all, just water racing past like it was going somewhere and needed to get there in a hurry. Like it wanted to take us all on that raft and make us ride with it, faster and faster, wherever it wanted to take us.

CHAPTER 5

Cloudland

Beck

Music is thumping, bass heavy and almost visible on the cloud of smoke swirling around the entrance to the gig. As soon as I get inside, the slime of three hundred dancing people's sweat and the stink of cigarettes saturate my skin. I grin at Pete. It smells like a great night. The floor is slippery with spilt drinks and spew, and it's only half-past eight. Best of all, no one even checks our dodgy ID cards. The suspension dance floor is bouncing to the thud of stomping boots and a couple of fellas are mid-brawl near one of the bars, surrounded by a circle of shouting, clapping onlookers.

Angie and I edge our way around the fight to the loo. My bladder feels like a water balloon and makeup is dribbling down my chin. Sweat oozes behind my knees into my tights as I ease them down so I can pee. My black velvet dress clings to my back and droplets of milky, foundation-stained perspiration drip from my nose. Sure the floral halter-neck dress my mother wanted me to wear would've been more appropriate, weather-wise, but I'd rather be dead than be seen in that thing. She's got no idea.

I exhale menthol smoke and wipe at my face with satin gloves before chucking the butt in the bowl. It's hard to look good in Brisbane.

Out at the basins I re-fluff my hair to stop the daggy effect of the damp, redo my eyeliner and lips with the same black pencil, and practise hard looks in the mirror. But no matter how thickly I paint my mask, on the inside I still feel small and lonely.

'Do I look okay?' I check with Angie.

She wolf-whistles then says, 'Watch out Pete.'

She knows how much I like him. He's sexier than Orlando Bloom.

She also knows my most embarrassing secret. I'm a kiss-virgin. Fifteen and never had a proper kiss. Well, I did kiss Douggie from down the road once, at a party when I was thirteen, but it was playing spin-the-bottle so it doesn't count. And Douggie, URGH! Tonight though, I'm in with a real chance. Pete and I have been really close lately, always holding hands and stuff. Sure he says he's gay, but that's just because he hasn't kissed me yet. If only he'd let me, I'd drift away on his dreamy grey eyes forever. I make a vow to myself that I'll kiss him before the night is over.

Angie and I weave our way across the seasick dance floor to where the boys are waiting. They're near the right hand speaker in front of the stage. It's our pre-arranged meeting place, where everyone from school is hanging out, everyone who wants to party. The boys in torn jeans and t-shirts, with packets of smokes rolled up in their sleeves, showing off their muscles; the skins in Docs and braces; the folkies with dreadlocks, green teeth and the best dope; the surfies in board shorts and peroxided hair; the sluts with big boofy hairdos and pierced bellybuttons, trying to come on to all of them. And us.

Screaming at the top of her lungs like her guts are about to bust, a rock chick is flashing her undies, doing high kicks in her old school uniform, gripping onto a glowing fluoro tube.

'Hey!' I shout at Pete, my lips tickling his ear. 'It's her. She stole the light from my kitchen.' We cack ourselves, holding each other and rolling on the floor. I almost kiss him then, while we're laughing.

He grew up on a farm. He's Catholic. He kills cane toads with his bare hands, for God's sake. He can't really be gay.

Our cheeks touch and I turn my head so that my lips are almost there. But then Jase turns up with Cokes he's topped up with gin. He leans over and gives Angie a big pash. She doesn't look happy about him smearing her lipstick but I'd do anything for a kiss like that. Long and wet and wild. I glance over at Pete, my heart beating out hope in Morse code.

'Hey! Stop that you two. That's disgusting. Bloody heteros,' he says, getting to his feet.

I swallow hard. He doesn't mean it, it's just a cover for, for... well anyway, I'm not going to give up.

I throw my bag into the corner behind the speaker where the bottle of gin is stashed, so I can dance. Everyone's going crazy, throwing themselves around, limbs flailing, animal dancing. But not us. Pete and I hold hands and do the careful in-together, out-together move from the film clip we really like, while Angie and Jase practise neat controlled pogoing mixed in with some robotic arm moves.

It feels good to dance with Pete, touching him, feeling the softness of his hands. But more than that. To dance all together, as part of a mass of sweating moving bodies. All of us out of it. All of us young. Ecstatic faces turned towards the band, smiles plastered, eyes closed, hair spraying sweat.

This is our ball.

I step back and bump into Brian, Douggie's brother. They live just down the road from my place, and my brother Russ is in their gang. I've known them since forever, though we've never really hung out. Brian's not a bad guy but I hate the way he stares at me, like he's starving to death and I'm a burger with the works. We score dope from him sometimes. 'Hey,' I say.

'Hey!' he bellows. 'Great isn't it?'

'Too right.'

All his gang are here, cool guys, druggies and rev-heads. There's Russ, though as usual he's pretending I don't exist, Steve, Jacko. But no Douggie. There've been some rumours about him; people say he's flipped out.

Jacko is dancing like a lunatic, throwing his head around, his long hair stinging anyone who gets too close. He's dancing like he's angry with his body, like he hates it, beating himself with his fists.

I realise I've stopped dancing and that I'm staring at him, wondering about him. He's not at school anymore. Mum gets petrol at the garage where he works. He's tough and really sexy in that leather jacket he always wears, big shoulders and a tight little arse in his jeans. Everyone looks up to him. He's been the king of our neighbourhood since I was ten. I haven't seen him around much lately though, and when I do he looks totally wasted, with his mouth set in a grimace and pulled down hard in the corners.

He must feel me staring because he stops dancing, stands still among the threshing bodies. Stops. And looks at me.

Pete taps me on the back. 'Joint time hey?'

'Sure.' The second band is setting up so there's plenty of time for a smoke outside before they come on. We grab Angie and Jase and climb the stairs to the upper floor, making our way out past the stalls into the fresh air on the balcony. The night air is cool on our sweaty skin. I wish Pete would put his arm around me. I try to snuggle my back into him as he leans against the wall, but he edges away.

Jase pulls out a couple of squished joints from his pocket, smooths one into shape and lights up. I'm pretty drunk. Dancing has sent the gin racing through my bloodstream so one puff on the joint starts my head spinning. I keep quiet, pass it on and should know better than to take it back. But I do and that's it.

'Urk,' I groan. 'I'm going to spew.'

'Shit, not again. Vomit Queen.' Jase is disgusted. 'Give the joint to me, don't get chuck all over it.'

He tokes the guts out of it and flicks the roach over the railing. Sparks fly and the glow of the embers descends in an arc, past the lights of the city, all the way to the ground.

'Come on,' he says to Angie. 'I'm not hanging around to watch Beck lose her lunch. The band will be almost finished by the time we get down. Let's go muscle in; get a good spot right up the front. We'll wait for you guys there, okay?'

'Sure. I'm coming in a minute. Just got to get it out then I'll be right.'

I can tell Pete wants to go too. He keeps tapping his feet and looking through the doorway even while he pats me on the shoulder.

This isn't going to be the night. There's no way he'll want to kiss me with vomit on my breath.

No one will.

'Go on, I'll be okay. I'm an expert. Just let me spew in peace.'

'You sure?'

'Go. Get out of here. I can't hold it.' There's an awful sweetness at the back of my throat.

'I've seen you chuck before.'

'I know. You laughed.'

'Alright then. But if you're not down by the time the main band comes on, I'm coming to get you.'

'Promise?'

'Promise.'

And promise you'll kiss me and be mine forever? But I don't say it out loud; just think it so hard it makes my head ache.

He goes, leaving me clinging to the railing, spinning, waiting for the vomit to make that final leap up my throat. My gullet opens and, like a black fountain, the gin and coke and Mum's spaghetti come flying out, making a loud splash on the cement below. I heave again and again, getting some in my hair.

'Spewing hey?'

'Yeah. Go away.'

'Want a drink?'

Who is that? I wipe my mouth with the back of my hand and turn. It's Jacko in his leather jacket, holding a can of XXXX out to me.

'Urgh, not beer. Don't suppose you've got any water?'

'Hang on a tick.' He saunters off down the stairs. I don't expect to see him again, let alone get any water. I spit and cough and try to empty the last of the gin out of my guts. That's it. I'm never drinking again.

He comes back. 'Here you are,' he says handing me his beer can. 'Don't worry it's water. Filled it up in the dunnies.'

'Thanks.' I take a swig, rinse, gargle and spit. 'Don't look.' Not the best thing to do in front of the hottest boy in the neighbourhood, but it has to be done.

I splash the vomit out of my hair but the smell still hangs around. I drink some water, let it settle, and when I feel like nothing else is going to come up, I turn and hold out the can.

'Here you are. Sorry about the spew germs.'

'Keep it.'

'Thanks.'

Neither of us says anything for about five minutes. He just keeps staring at me with a puzzled look in his eyes, like he's trying to figure something out. The air around us feels hard. I have to say something.

'Got a cigarette?' What else do you say to a guy to keep him around? What's he doing up on the balcony alone anyway? Why's he hanging around me?

'You sure you want to smoke after you've just chucked?'

'Yeah. I'll be fine now. It was the gin that did it.'

'Yeah. Gin rots your guts. Metho.'

'So, have you got a smoke?'

'Sure.' He pulls a crumpled packet of cigarettes out of his jeans' pocket and flips up the lid. 'There's only one left.'

'Oh. It's alright then.'

'We can share it.'

It feels weird putting the cigarette to my lips and having him strike a match under my nose, cupping his hands against the wind and holding the flame there long after the cigarette's alight, looking at my face like he's never seen it before.

'You're really white, aren't you?' He usually has some roast-chook-brown surfie chick hanging on his arm, never the same one for very long. But lately there hasn't seemed to be anyone.

I pass the cigarette over. 'I'm Beck. Rebecca. Remember?'

'Jack. Everyone calls me Jacko.'

'I know. I live down the street from Brian and Douggie.'

He looks confused.

'Near the creek. Russ's sister?'

Then it clicks.

'Shit really? Hang on. Now I've got you.' He takes a step back, nodding and smiling like he's got a good secret. 'I know you. Wasn't your hair red?'

'How embarrassing.' I take the cigarette back from him, brushing fingertips. I shiver.

'Why do you want to go and make yourself look freaky like that?'

'I think I look good.' I don't want to share anything with him anymore. He obviously doesn't understand.

'I just mean, I reckon you'd look okay if you toned it down a bit. Like what's with the black stuff round your eyes?' He licks his finger and wipes off a smudge of kohl pencil from under my eye. His fingertip feels warm. 'And I mean, black lips? What's that about?' He's staring at my mouth.

'I don't suppose you've heard of Marilyn Manson,' I sniff, turning my head away.

'Yeah, yeah. I've heard of him. He's arse-ugly, man. He needs it. But you, you're okay, you don't need to hide behind all that shit.'

I suck hard on the butt, torn between being insulted and flattered. I pass back the cigarette and look up at him through the smoke, letting the silence and the whorls of grey hang between us till I think of something to say.

'So what's your story anyway? Why aren't you downstairs with your mates?'

'I'm tired of all their bullshit. I just wanted to be alone.'

'Till you caught me spewing my guts out.'

'Yeah. But it's sort of like being alone.'

'Thanks.'

'Hey don't get all huffy. I just meant you're alright. You know, easy to talk to.'

I take back the butt and burn my finger. 'Ouch!' I put it in my mouth.

He takes it out and kisses it better.

I wrench my hand away. 'What is it with you? What do you want?'

'Nothing. I ... Just ...'

'What's the matter?'

He shakes his head, with his mouth turned down.

'Is it your mum?' More than once his mother's turned up on Angie's doorstep in the middle of the night, bashed and bleeding from fights with his father. She always goes back though.

'What the fuck do you know about my mother?'

I've said the wrong thing.

'Nothing, nothing. Angie's mum knows her that's all. You know, about the fighting and stuff.'

'She doesn't know anything about my family, all right? It's none of her fucking business.'

'Is it bad?'

He doesn't say anything but he nods; a small nod like someone invisible is holding his head and forcing him.

He's standing so close to me I can feel the heat from his jeans and jacket oozing across to my body, and with it the weight of his heart. I stretch out my little finger and touch his hand next to mine on the railing.

'I'm sorry.'

'Don't be.'

I put my small white hand on his big brown one and hold it there.

And suddenly he pulls me to him and plants his lips on mine and I taste the salt of his sweat and the whisky he's drunk and the Winfields he's smoked and the deep, tough wildness of him. And he keeps kissing me and kissing me as if he's trying to swallow me whole, taking breath from me, till I feel like I'm drowning in his pain.

'Hey,' I say pulling away. 'Stop. I can't breathe.'

'Sorry,' he says. 'Come on, Beck. I really want to.'

The bass line of the main band's first song starts moaning out from below.

'You don't know me.'

'Come on.'

Pete's head appears at the doorway, his eyebrows raised, ready to come to my rescue. But I wave him away with hands still wrapped around Jacko; watch as he makes an 'Ooh Ah' face and skips down the stairs dying to tell someone.

Jacko looks around. 'Who was that?'

'No one,' I say. 'Come here.'

And I pull him closer, standing on tiptoe to press my lips to his.

Softly.

CHAPTER 6
The River

Brian

I suppose everything started to really turn to shit last summer when Jacko turned eighteen and bought his bomb of a car. Not that I'm blaming him. It was all that stupid wine company's fault. If they hadn't put a 'Scratch and Win' ticket with a ten thousand dollar prize in every four-litre cask, none of it would have ever happened. Or maybe it would have, just not so fast and all at once. To us Oxley Creek Boys, it was like a message from God, giving us a job to do, a purpose. Sort of like that bloke in France they told us about in school. He got a letter from Jesus telling him to get a bunch of kids together to go fight a crusade.

We didn't have a war to go to like they did. But we got our message just the same.

Ever since I can remember we've been the Oxley Creek Boys, since even before we made our raft – Jacko, Douggie, Russ, Steve, and me. We used to fly up planks of wood on our BMX bikes, leap over buckets and burst through walls of hose-spray. We rattled down the hill on brakeless go-carts and crashed into the gully, coming up bloody but laughing. Sometimes we got hurt, a broken arm or bad gravel rash, but never anything that couldn't be fixed and never anything that stopped us doing it all over again.

'I dare ya,' was our motto.

Once we hit high school, we found out there were more things to try. Everyone was smoking dope – well all the cool kids anyway, the ones that mattered. We made our first bongs out of juice bottles and bits of hose, and cones from tinfoil. We pooled our money from part-time jobs and paper runs and bought huge bags of grass, smoking it in endless weekend sessions, pulling cone after cone, laughing and coughing and gorging on junk food, till we ended up in a sweaty heap on the cubby floor, empty wrappers stuck to our backs, staring into space unable to speak.

We tried magic mushrooms, acid, nitrous oxide, pills – whatever we could get our hands on. Wc laughed all the time, especially at Douggie's jokes. Mostly we laughed about other people who weren't as cool as us. Life was a party and we partied harder than anyone.

One drunken night we decided that those 'Scratch and Win' tickets in the casks were the best way for us to get rich, as well as getting us a place in the world record books as unbeatable drinking thrill seekers. Our crusade. We wanted to be the coolest, and that meant being able to drink everyone else under the table. So we made a pact to drink a four-litre cask of wine a day, each, until we won. Moselle. Goon.

Money wasn't a problem. Jacko and me both had jobs at the local servo by then, and Steve and Douggie did papers. The rest of our cash came from selling dope at school to kids who didn't know any better.

We drank the goon straight in tumblers, in mugs with ice, blended into smoothies with apple and even banana. Though I only tried banana once. It made me chuck. We drank it lukewarm and heated up over campfires on cold winter nights. We weren't just any old drinkers – we were the 'Goon Babies'. At night, huddled around the heater in the cubby, we sang hymns about goon like those French kids probably sang about Jesus. My favourite was sung to the tune of Gloria and went like this, 'Goo-oo-oo-oo-ooniie, we shall drink forever,' over and over again. We had a great time, arms around each other, swaying together, warm inside and out. Friends forever. Champion thrill seekers. Just like when we were kids.

Sometimes we won another cask of goon with our lucky tickets, but never the money.

So we kept trying. And trying. We couldn't believe it when yet another scratchie came up with 'Better luck next time'. It became the goon marathon, dragging on over months, straggling into the new year. Those French kids kept on marching to prove themselves, to serve their God. We served ours too. No giving up. Not ever. Anyway, we were having too much fun.

On the weekends when other part-time goon babies joined us, we had crazy boat adventures. In Dad's old tin dinghy we puttered down the polluted creek into the river, dodging barges, the occasional cruiser, and the dredges that made the river such a murky brown. There was a cement pontoon under the Indooroopilly Bridge where we left the boat while we scrambled up the bank through mangroves and lantana to the road. Half-swaggering, half-stumbling, we made our way to the orange brick pub and stocked up on supplies.

One Friday night, as we were tying up at the pontoon, I spotted a Russian wolfhound that was stuck in the mud. The dog's long hair was black and stinking, hanging from its loose skin. Even in the dark, his eyes gave me the spooks. They looked empty, like he'd given up hope. Like we were too late. He didn't even have the strength to move his legs and help us as we heaved, pulling him free of the black gunge that had sucked him in so deep only his front legs and head were still out.

We got him into the boat and went straight home, where we dragged him into the back seat of Jacko's car on a beach towel and drove to the free vet clinic at the Uni, his head bouncing on my lap. For a big dog he was really light. At the clinic they took him from my arms, put him on a trolley and wheeled him away. I swear he turned and looked at me.

The next afternoon I went to visit but he'd died in the morning. The vet said he'd been stuck in the mud a long time, a week or more. All they'd found in his stomach were a few yabbies. I felt real bad then. He shouldn't have died. I should've found him sooner. I'll never forget that look he gave me. I should've known then it was a sign. A warning.

The weekend after we found the dog, we snuck into the Sea Scouts' shed and borrowed a bigger boat so we could fit everyone in. We had four extras that night. Everyone wanted to be in on our fun. First stop was the Indooroopilly golf course just up from where the creek joined the river. We pulled the boat onto mud at the bottom of a cliff and climbed up the bank to one side of the cliff face. We collected flags from holes as souvenirs and wandered around, so wasted that we were never all standing at the same time. It was a beautiful night. We laughed and sang our goon songs to the moon.

Across the river the powerhouse was sparkling with lights like a space-age city, its chimneys reaching high and smoky. It looked like magic, the Promised Land, so we headed in that direction. But first we had to find the boat, down on the mud far below. As usual Jacko led the way. He reckoned we wouldn't even know how to scratch our own arses if he didn't show us how.

'This way,' he called, leading us down a path, then disappearing.

I followed straight after him.

The track ended with a step into darkness, a couple of seconds' wingless flight, and a hard thumping body-slam flat into the mud.

'Don't come this way,' I yelled up to the fellas. But no one heard, and even if they had, they probably would still have followed. That's what mates did. Soldiers follow their leader.

One by one they fell the ten-metre drop off the cliff to the riverbank.

Because we were so out of it we landed soft and floppy in the mud and no one got hurt. The glass bong in Steve's hand got smashed but he didn't even cut himself. A miracle. It was a hell of a drop. We wiped off a bit of the mud, laughed, and had another drink to celebrate. Back in the boat, I started the motor and we crossed the night-dark river to the lights of the powerhouse.

It seemed empty so we went inside, whispering at first, getting louder when no alarm bells rang and no guards appeared. We opened the workmen's lockers and helped ourselves to their dinner-box sandwiches and biscuits; made a bonfire of their magazines and books to keep warm. Jacko figured out how to get inside a crane, so we mucked around with that for a while. Douggie fell asleep in the boat. Russ went to explore further into the enormous building and got lost, returning hours later with a sketched map and the autograph of a worker who'd given him directions back out.

The sky was starting to brighten by then, so we headed back to the scout hut to return the boat. We were polishing off the last of the bottles and dancing with muddy boots on the narrow bunks when the scoutmaster arrived. He went ballistic and yelled at us till his face went red. But we weren't afraid. We knew he was the one who practised his knot tying around little boys' willies. Old perve. We got out of there quick-smart anyway, leaving him wiping mud off the vinyl mattress covers.

Back home we squashed into Jacko's car, chucking the young ones in the boot, and hit the pub for some beer. We drove to the local park of steep green hills and fig trees by the curve of the river, and found ourselves a comfortable spot for our beer breakfast picnic. The first beers were delicious, cold and refreshing, but no one finished their second, all of us finally falling asleep in the hard white glare of the morning sun.

When I woke up happy families were spreading picnic blankets around us, unpacking hampers, keeping their kids close by. I felt dirty, covered in mud and soaked to the core in goon. Douggie was crying.

The next weekend he had his fight with Steve.

But that didn't stop us drinking. The goon marathon has stretched on and on, I don't think it'll ever end. Jacko's moved out and got a place of his own where I hang out most of the time, away from Mum's tears and Douggie's crazy talk. We party every night, and every weekend the house overflows with kids who want to be us. But I can't get a handle on it anymore. Nothing's easy like it was before. Nothing's fun. All the promises we made of undying friendship have turned to shit and everyone's changed. Not just Douggie either. Feels like that bloody mud's got us all neck deep, grasping for the mangroves to pull ourselves out.

It's every man for himself.

And for all our drinking we've never won a cent. I wonder if there even is a prize. I've been thinking about those French kids on their crusade a lot lately, too. Tramping over snowy mountains singing their stupid songs, till they froze and starved, heading towards something that didn't really exist. You know what happened to them in the end? The ones that didn't die getting to the port were sold into slavery. Not one of them made it to the Promised Land. Not one.

CHAPTER 7
Joint Effort

Douggie

I like girls. I like everything about them – how their hair smells clean, how their legs feel after they've shaved them, the way they're round in parts I'm flat. Their lips. The way they press hard against me as they're about to come. They can't get enough of me and my banana dick either. The Sex God of Brisbane, here to serve.

I've been home a couple of months taking the bloody pills the doctor at the hospital gave me like a good little boy. Mum watches me in the mornings over our cereal, making sure I swallow them down. Maybe they're helping, maybe not. There was nothing wrong with me in the first place, except for a couple of paranoid nights on the smoke. I keep telling Brian that, over and over, but he and the other fellas still act as if I've got something worse than leprosy. Jealous as hell. I'm not worried, lots of other famous guys have the same trouble. I suppose they're scared that if I turn up at parties they won't get a look in with the girls.

They're not going to stop me going out though. I've got as much right to fun as anyone. More. Tonight I'm off to a Joint Effort, a gig at the Uni, lots of bands, heaps of chicks, sweaty and hot, just begging for it.

———

I lie down on the floor to zip up my daks, the tightest black jeans you've ever seen. They make my arse irresistible. Slip on my new purple shirt, do my eyeliner and I'm ready. I have to take the bus. Brian and the others took off in the tinny before, snuck down to the cubby and didn't think I'd notice. But I saw them – I heard the motor roaring out into the creek – and I know exactly where they're going. Too bad for them if I root all the girls before they even get there.

I listen to some Mental as Anything songs on the bus on the way to the Uni. Old fart stuff I know, but still cool. My favourite is 'The Nips are Getting Bigger'. I reckon it's about girls' tits growing. That's what I sing anyway 'Uh hoh, the tits are getting bigger'. I like tits – round ones, small ones, perky, droopy, pointy, all of them. Everyone on the bus is checking me out; reckon they must recognise me from the telly. I give them a free concert all the way in. Guess I'm feeling generous.

Life's pretty good when you don't think about all the shit, like not having a dad, and Mum losing the plot. Brian not being around much anymore. When I've got my music, some pot and the promise of girls, it feels like anything is possible. Maybe this is how Jesus felt when he was about to raise that guy from the dead. Like a miracle is just around the corner. God energy is filling me up as I belt out the last song and get off the bus to a round of applause. Tonight I'm invincible.

As I walk across the sandstone court towards the lights and music I straighten myself up, make sure I'm looking good. I drag a comb through my hair and wipe my shoes clean, smooth my shirt across my chest and practise my pout.

At the gate they question my ID but I joke with them about how people do that all the time and how really I'm twenty, and they let me in. You'd think they'd let someone as famous as me in for free. They'll probably want me to get up and do a song or two later.

My heart starts beating faster as I head into the crowd, moving closer to the music. Guitar riffs are blaring from huge speakers and chicks are already screaming. Concerts are great; the girls are always revved up and excited. All that dancing and making eyes at the band gets them in the mood.

Heaps of roughnecks are bouncing around like pogo sticks, pretty mean looking, with safety pin earrings and rips in their clothes, and lots of shaved heads. Most of them are totally wasted. The band looks wild too, and real angry. They sound okay. Loud enough that's for sure.

I thread my way through sweating bodies, following a guy with a Mohican to near the right hand speaker, where the gang always hangs at gigs. A whole pile of kids from school are there, thrashing around, having a good time. That's the good thing about living in a hole like Brisbane – there are so few things to do that at least when there is something worth going to, everyone you know turns up too.

Jacko's already here, doing deals, yelling into people's ears, handing over joints and shoving money in his pocket. Russ's sister Beck is hanging off his arm like she'll never let him go. How she ended up with him I'll never know. She's all right. Used to be too daggy for me but now it looks like she's loosened up a bit. I flash her a look and she smiles back. She remembers. We were in the same class in grade seven; I used to pay out on her something terrible. Kissed her once too. Wasn't bad.

I push my way past Russ, to where Brian is trying to pogo, looking like a beanbag being dropped from a height every time he lands and splattering everyone around him with a mixture of sweat and mud. Steve's playing air guitar next to him.

'Hey Brian!' I yell into his hair as I come up behind him.

'What the? Fuck. What're you doing here?'

'Free country isn't it?'

'Shit. Just don't do anything stupid all right? Nothing freaky. Did you take your pills today?'

'For fuck's sake, one mother's enough. I'm going to have a good time tonight that's all. If you don't like it well, sucko.'

'Okay, okay. Just don't...'

'What?'

'You know.'

I play it cool for a while, sort of rocking a bit, moving my hips but not much else as I grin around at the girls from school. A few of them nod back but most of them grab their girlfriend's hands and turn away, shouting into each other's ears.

'I'm going up the front to check out the groupies,' I tell Brian. 'Want to come?'

'No way. I'm staying here with Jacko and Beck. You go if you want. But remember what I said, no freaky stuff,' he yells back.

I don't bother asking Steve. He moved away as soon as he saw me coming.

So I elbow through the thrashing moshpit to where the front line of punters are squashed up against the stage and press myself between a couple of cute chicks. One turns, angry that I've muscled in at first, but when I wink and mouth 'hi', she smiles. I use the force of the crowd to lean against her and she doesn't even try to move away. I'm on.

By the time the set finishes I've got my arm around the girl and we're heading to the dunnies for a joint. A joint's always good bait. Rooting and fishing have a lot in common really and I reckon this one's dying to get caught. Her tits, big and bouncy and shining with sweat, are almost falling out of her skull t-shirt, it's cut so low. She sure is up for it – already sliding her hand under my shirt and feeling my skin. And she's totally out of it. Don't know what she's on but I wouldn't mind some.

As we pass Brian on our way out the side of the crowd, I give him a quick nod. He looks like he could spew he's so jealous. I reckon he's probably never even had a root, too fat and spotty. I could teach him a trick or two if he'd just shut up and listen for a change.

I take the girl to the dunnies out the back. It's quieter there. As I lead her past the dudes at the trough, someone I don't even know calls out, 'Go for it mate!'

'Don't pay any attention to him,' I say as I open a cubicle door and usher her inside. I turn the lock to 'engaged' and light up, pretending that we both don't know we're here for other things than the smoke. 'So, what's your name?'

'Amanda, but call me Mandy, everyone does.'

'You're real pretty, Mandy.'

She grins, showing a gold tooth at the front. Her pupils are huge, and in the bright light of the cubicle I realise that her eyelashes aren't real and that she's a lot older than I thought – maybe even twenty-five.

'Come here then,' I say and put the lit end of the joint in my mouth, giving her the filter to suck on as I blow, a classic shotty. By the time we've smoked the joint down to a roach our lips will be touching. I've used the old shotty line a million times. It never fails. Her lipstick-red lips close around the joint but I must blow too hard because she coughs and pulls away spluttering.

'Are you okay?'

'I'll be alright in a minute.' She chucks the rest of the joint into the toilet even though there's heaps left, grabs my jeans by the belt loops and pulls me to her till her hipbones are grinding into my thighs. She plants a wet one on me, sticking her tongue so far down my throat I gag. She's no virgin this one. I'm in like Flynn, she's clawed open my daks, and is scratching at my balls. We do it wild and furious against the wall.

Afterwards, as we walk back up the stairs to the band, she wants to hold my hand but I need both of them to do up my zip. As soon as we're into the crowd I head back to the others and give her the slip. Once was enough with her. Fierce.

I'm dancing away next to Brian minding my own business when she appears like a witch out of nowhere. She's clutching the hand of a pudgy looking skinhead.

'That's him,' she screeches pointing at me. 'What are you going to do about it?' I don't even have a chance to say anything in my defence before the skin's whacked into me.

'What's your problem mate?' I yell as I reel backwards into the safety cushion that is Brian. 'She was all over me.'

But he's not listening. 'As if she'd be into you, ya scrawny little dickhead.' He kicks out with his steel capped boot and brings me to my knees.

Then another skin appears, towering over his mate.

It's on. So I roar like I really am crazy and hurl myself at the short one, pummelling sharp punches to the guts.

Brian grabs at the other guy to try to keep him off, but it's too late. The big rocker starts in on me too and then three more skins join in. Steve, Russ and Jacko come running. Thank God for big mates.

'Fucking hell Douggie, haven't I told you never to pick skins?' grunts Brian between punches. He's tackling one fella around the waist as he kicks at the short one who's got me on the floor. I don't have the breath to explain as I try to roll out from under, spitting into the guy's face.

Jacko grabs the small skin's braces and drags him off me, hurling him into the crowd. Then Steve tackles the big one and gives him a quick punch to the guts that has him gasping for air.

Jacko yells 'FIGHT!' and starts kung fu kicking like a mad man. Beck screams and runs out of the line of fire. Everyone else mucks in. Massive, pig-dog ugly bald guys come at us from all directions. It's a free for all. Fun – except when that big guy lands a fist in my ear. The music is loud and frantic. I punch in time with the beat. Smack. Bang. Wallop. I feel like Batman doing Kapow hits till a bouncer throws a heavy elbow into my face and chucks me against the wall. Bloody Beck must've got the bouncers.

Shit. My nose is bleeding. Better not be broken.

Jacko slams one last punch into a skin's head then yells, 'Go! Everyone out of here. GO! Down to the boat!' He runs for the balcony without even a look to see if anyone is following, and hurdles over the railing, disappearing with a metallic thud onto a van below. Brian grabs my shirt and hauls me off the fella I was wrestling, lugging me out the side door. Steve overtakes. I laugh, pumped full of adrenaline. But the skins are just as wired. And they're after us. The fellas hurl themselves over the railing, crashing and rolling onto the van's roof. Just before I jump I look behind and see Beck calling out for Jacko. But he's long gone.

'Jump Beck! Come on!' shouts Brian from below. 'Let's get out of here.'

She tumbles down after me, falling off the van into the carpark and we bolt through the trees after the others. The thunder of heavy boots drops onto metal a few seconds after us. Way too close.

'RUN!' I roar at Beck's back. 'They're coming!'

Like stampeding elephants, the skins give chase, yelling threats and throwing beer cans. One whacks me on the back of the head but I don't even look around. I keep running even though I've got a stitch. My legs are burning. I grip at my side and turn my head to see if I can slow down but there are at least twenty furious skinheads charging after me.

'Fuck!' I scream. 'Faster! They're gaining on us.'

I clutch at Beck's arm. She's panting and starting to get the trembles so I call out to Brian, who half carries her the rest of the way to the pontoon. Jacko's already in the boat pulling like a maniac on the starter cord. He barely even looks up as Beck collapses into the dinghy. The motor splutters then conks.

'Jesus! Give me a go!' yells Brian, as we leap in from the jetty. 'They're right behind us. Get in! Hurry!'

Russ jumps in, almost tipping us, followed by Steve who trips on a nail and tumbles in on his back. The engine's still conking.

Zip, putter, putter, putt.

'Shit! Shit!' chants Brian as he tries again.

The skins are on the pontoon. One of them is waving a broken bottle over his head.

'Do it!'

'FUCK!'

Steve unties the rope and grabs an oar. I scramble for the other one and we start paddling as fast as we can away from the jetty. But not fast enough. A huge guy vaults into the boat onto me but I whack him with the oar. The motor roars into action and the boat swerves out into the river, toppling the skinhead into the water. He comes up swearing at the top of his lungs. Behind him, the pontoon sags with the weight of the rockers who are foaming at the mouth, they're so angry. They promise certain death and throw cans, bottles, and rocks into the wash behind us as the dinghy zooms away.

We laugh with relief, panting and slapping each other on the back. Sweaty, bloody, exhilarated.

'That was too close for comfort,' I say, watching as the skins rock a parked car onto its side and start flipping it towards the river. 'They were some mean bastards.'

'Are you kidding? That was fucken unreal!' raves Jacko from where he's regained control of the rudder. Beck is crammed in beside him, stuck to his hip. 'Best fight we've had in ages.'

'Yeah,' the fellas answer, echoing Jacko like they always do.

'Did you see the way I dropped that midget one upside down?' Jacko asks and then we re-live every punch and kick, making ourselves the heroes of the story. I scoop up some water and splash my face, checking my nose and sore ear.

'Reckon I'm going to have a black eye in the morning,' I say. Everyone has some wound to show off. We compete to see whose is worst. Steve might have broken a rib but he says it's nothing. Brian's got a fat lip and

Russ's chipped half a tooth off so he looks real freaky when he smiles.

'What was that skinhead's problem anyway?' Brian asks.

'Shit, that doesn't matter, does it Douggie?' says Jacko. 'We had a great night, didn't we?'

It's a long way home and all the booze is gone. In the cold, my muscles start to ache and my nose is throbbing. I hope it's not going to mend crooked. No fight's worth losing my looks for. My face is my passport. My fame depends on it.

Empty goon bladders and crumpled cigarette packets slosh around my feet as the dinghy speeds down the middle of the river towards home. The water looks like milk, with the full moon shining on it, almost beautiful when you can't see the dirt. Brian blows up one of the silver bladders and drops it overboard and we watch as it floats away, glowing like an astronaut's balloon in space. That'd be the way to go, just float away and never come back. Away from all the shit. Maybe I'd see Dad there at the end of the Universe. Maybe.

But if I start thinking like that I'm going nowhere. It's been a great night, feels like one of the old boat adventures before everyone started going weird on me. So I reckon I'll cheer us all up with one of my songs. I've got some lyrics that kill. The angels sing them in my ear sometimes when I'm stoned like I am now. Like...

Flying / Flying away with you /You and me Babe / Yeah.

Pretty good, hey?

I try it out, singing into the wind and it sounds unreal.

Behind me I hear them all laughing. Laughing and whispering, 'Crazy Douggie'. But tonight it's different, they're laughing with me. Or it feels like they are anyway.

This is the song that's going to make my first million. Number one with a rocket. Fellas shouting my name and all the girls screaming and fainting as I stride out on stage into the flashing lights, my leather pants tight and sexy, my silver jacket reflecting colours. One girl jumps up on stage, even before I sing the first line and bouncers drag her kicking and fighting to the side. Her skirt gets hitched right up and I see her undies, 'Douggie 4 eva' written in felt pen on her crotch. I blow her a kiss and start to sing, the microphone rough against my lips.

I belt it out and stare into the camera, doing 'fuck me' eyes like I practise in front of the mirror. I fall onto my knees and sing, 'Baby, baby. I want you so bad,' reaching out my hand to touch the fingertips of screaming fans. A couple of them faint and have to be carried away on stretchers. I start to get up, putting one foot on the front of the boat. The wind feels great as it rushes past.

'Hey Douggie! Watch it!'

The boat tips to one side as I balance on the prow.

'Flying away with me,' I sing, then yell out to the fellas behind me, 'Check this out!' And I put the other foot on the metal and lean forward with my hands on the point of the boat till I can stand upright. I put my arms out to the sides to balance and sing, 'Flying! Flying!' The climax of the song. The crowd roars!

'For fuck's sake Douggie, sit down!' Jacko shouts.

He's not that into my music.

'Okay, okay,' I mutter, but I could've stayed like that the whole way home, face into the wind, cool and sexy.

I reach down a hand onto the boat's nose but I slip and land with a thud on my arse. Water starts flooding over the front and side. Cold.

The fellas start hollering. 'Move back! Lean left! Lean left!' But it's too late. The river's taking over the boat; we're sinking faster than the Titanic. We're all in the drink, floundering like catfish on the end of a line.

I start swimming like crazy. Luckily we're not too far out. My jeans drag on my legs but I'm a pretty good swimmer, got a trophy last year at school, so I make it to the bank first.

Steve crawls up out of the mud and punches me on the arm, 'You big loser. Why'd you have to go and do that for? We could've drowned.'

'What? What did I do?'

It's not really a question he's supposed to answer so I look out at the others struggling in with the boat. Brian's helping Beck to hang onto the side as he and Russ kick it in. And then I see Jacko clambering up out of the mud. At least I think it's Jacko. Jacko with no clothes on, stark white and skinny, dragging his jacket behind him. His droopy grey undies sagging and leaving a trail of drips.

I turn to Steve and grin and he smiles right back at me, like maybe he's even missed me a bit.

'It was worth it,' he says and we laugh till we could bust.

CHAPTER 8
Mates and Mushrooms

Brian

I saw Russ last night. He came to me in my dream. Funny that, how the dead come to visit you in dreams. It freaked me out. Even though it's been months now since it happened, there he was, real as life. I could even smell the Marlboros on him, his hair as wild and bushy as it ever was.

'How's it going mate?' he said.

We were in that field, the one near the creek where we went picking mushies, a couple of weekends after the fight with the skins.

I didn't know what to say. What do you say to a dead guy?

'You look good, haven't changed a bit,' I said.

'Yeah mate, you look like a right bloody fat bastard.'

I laughed, 'Yeah mate, reckon I am.'

He was still the same funny bugger, always up for a laugh, when he wasn't having one of his moods that is. It was a shit of a thing. Should never have happened to him at all.

It was Jacko's idea to go mushy picking. We grabbed Steve and Russ on the way; at least we had the sense to leave Douggie at home. We were looking for gold tops. After that kid got sick that time, we steered clear of blue meanies. They weren't called mean for nothing. So gold tops it was. And we found them, heaps of them.

It'd rained the night before so we got up early and drove out to the vet school cow paddocks, down the creek a bit from Mum's. Grass seeds stuck to the hairs on our legs and our flip-flops got slippery with dew as we scoured the cow pats for mushies.

People always used to cheer when we arrived at parties with our shopping bags full of dripping black gold tops. Like at that coolest party ever at Jacko's place. That night we boiled up two huge vats of mushies, bubbling thick and black. Everyone had too much.

We tried to stop the little ones – the grommets – make them have only one cup; but shit, those mongrels, who could stop them? I didn't like to see the young ones get too wasted, not after what happened to Douggie. But you can't tell kids anything.

That was some party alright, chairs busting out through the windows onto the lawn, kids up trees howling at the moon, slam-dancing into walls. So many colours;

some wild trip. Then those fellas crashed and Jacko lost it, went ape-shit kicking their heads in till Russ and Steve threw the crashers out, and steered Jacko back to the dance floor.

That was just before the pigs came and that kid came running in screaming, 'The pigs, the fucken pigs. Anyone with drugs get out!'

We were out over the fence, across the neighbour's yard and hurtling down the street when we heard a sound like rolling drums, and there was the rest of the party racing down the asphalt after us. Don't know who was left back at the house, probably no one. That was some party. One of our great mushy parties.

There was going to be another one that night, that's why me and the other fellas were out there in the paddock, filling plastic bags, laughing and munching on a few as we went. Tasted foul, like rotten dirt, but still, we swallowed anything if it got us stoned.

The trip started coming on strong, good fresh mushies. They were always the best out in nature, with the trees and grass and everything. The clouds were going wild and we were laughing and falling over and forgetting what we were supposed to be doing.

'Fuck man, it's so fucken beautiful.'

That was Russ – he loved to be out in the bush, must've been the murri in him. He reckoned it was anyway, though he was so freckly I never would have guessed it. He could just walk up to cows and pat their slimy noses, laughing when they licked his face. He loved it out there. We were having a great time.

It was Jacko's idea to go for a swim. Swimming was magic when you were tripping. You know water and that, it's all over your skin, you swim in it, you drink it, but you can't breathe it. Sometimes that's a bit hard to remember.

So we went down to the creek. The rain had swelled it up and made it high and wide, rushing through the mangroves. It was swirling and exciting. We edged down the mud and took off our flip-flops.

'What are you waiting for, ya pussy?' said Jacko, even though he still had his shoes on. So I jumped right in.

And bugger me but that water was fierce. It was angry at me, wanted me down at the bottom sucking mud. I tried to swim back in but I couldn't. I was being dragged out into the middle. I started screaming, yelling for help.

Jacko stood on the bank laughing with Steve. They thought it was a joke.

Then Russ looked at me and I saw his face change. He pulled off his shirt and was in after me. He was a good swimmer, real strong. His arms were the biggest part of his body. His legs were stick thin, just waiting to catch up with his arms he reckoned. I was getting tired. My arms weren't big like his and they were hurting, burning, trying to fight through that heavy brown water.

'Mate,' I panted as he ploughed towards me.

'Don't worry Brian, I've got you.' He grabbed me round the waist and started pulling me back towards the bank.

Once he had me I stopped trying, let myself relax into the strength of his muscles dragging me forward, taking me home. He slowed down a bit, fighting against the current.

A log came rolling, tumbling towards us.

'Grab it! Grab the log!' he yelled, throwing me towards it. And I opened my eyes, remembered where I was, came back from the spa pool of my mushroom dreams, and reached for the rough bark as it rushed by. I held on good and tight, looked for Russ beside me. But he wasn't there.

He was back behind me still swimming for shore, his big freckly arms lifting out of the muddy swirl.

I gripped onto that log for dear life and floated down and down, all the way to the bridge where the log got snagged on a pylon. I pulled myself up onto the concrete slab at its base and huddled there, hanging onto the steel girder, shivering and freaking out till the water police came and got me.

They never found Russ though. Not ever. Not all those days they dragged the bottom and sent in divers. He just disappeared, lost in the dark mud of that fucking creek.

I used to think about him all the time, feel really bad about it. But Jacko says you can't let stuff like that get to you too much or you'll go crazy. So I try to forget about it, like he has. We never even talk about Russ anymore. Like he was never even here. I push what happened to the back of my mind, don't look Beck in the eye when she gets drunk and starts to cry. And whenever Russ's wonky-toothed grin flashes at me out of nowhere, or when the bloke in front of me in the queue at the fish and chip shop has the same big freckled arms, I close my eyes, shake my head and stuff it back down.

But then, last night, there he was. Large as life and grinning at me.

'Mate,' I said, 'I'm sorry.'

'You're right mate. You're right.'

'It should've been me.'

'Nah, mate, nah – it was always gunna be me.'

And he sort of patted me on the shoulder.

CHAPTER 9
Trouble

Brian

When the police car pulls up in the driveway at home a few weeks after that freaky dream, it's almost dawn. Kookaburras are laughing their heads off like it's any other day. If I'm lucky, Mum won't wake up to answer the door. But from where I'm sitting in the back, I see her already peeking out through the lounge room curtains. What the fuck am I going to say?

The pig beside me gets out and comes around to my door.

'Can't I just stay here?'

'Out.'

He keeps a firm grip on my arm as we trudge up the overgrown pathway, behind the other two cops.

They knock like only trouble can, hard and sharp, like gunshots.

I hear Mum inside rustling around, chucking things behind the couch. She's still tying the cord on her dressing gown, and smoothing back her hair into an elastic when she edges the door open.

'Mrs. Spencer?'

'Yes, that's me. That's my son Brian you've got there. Bri?' She holds out her hand towards me and I lift my eyes from my sneakers. Hope she can't tell I've been crying.

Mum leans towards me, her arms stretched wide and I'd do anything just to drop into them and hide. Be ten again and let her take care of everything. I step closer to her but the pig beside me drags me back. 'Hold your horses,' he says.

Mum frowns and puts her hands on her hips. 'What? What is it officer? What's he done?'

'There's been an incident, Mrs. Spencer. Brian here has been charged with possession of a prohibited substance and is due to appear in court day after tomorrow.' He checks his watch, 'Make that tomorrow, at ten. Do you take full responsibility for his attendance?'

'Incident? Illicit substance? What's going on? A bit of pot? Is that it? I know my boys have been dabbling but they're good boys really. You see they lost a good friend only a few months ago and their father...'

Oh shit, I hope she's not going to tell the whole bloody story, break down like she usually does.

'Mrs. Spencer I think we'd better come inside.'

'No. I don't think so. I know my rights. You just give me my boy and be on your way. I'll be ringing my lawyer about this.' She doesn't really have a lawyer but it sounds pretty good. 'Give me my boy.'

They let go of my shoulder and I let her hug me. Then something awful happens. I cry. Right there in front of the pigs. Can't help it. Mum only comes up to my chin these days but there's something about the way she holds me that makes me feel small. I struggle for breath, cling to her, trying to pull myself back together but I don't know whether that's possible. I feel like I'm a thousand piece jigsaw puzzle that's been tipped onto the floor. Who knows if all the pieces are still there? It's been one shit of a night. Once Mum finds out what I've done she may never hold me again.

She squints up at the police in the glare of the front-light.

'What's going on here? What've you done to my boy?'

'Just calm down, Mrs. Spencer. We really need to come inside. There's been an incident.'

'You already said that. What is it? What he's supposed to have done?'

'Mrs. Spencer, it's about your other son.'

'Doug?' she whispers. 'Douggie?' She sets her face for the worst, holding herself up on me. 'He's done it. He's dead.'

'No, Mrs. Spencer, he's not dead. It's not his life that's in jeopardy. There's been an incident, a serious incident. We really should come in.'

She tears me from her just like I knew she would. Shakes me. Hard. 'Where's your brother? Where's Douggie? What've you done? Can't you look after him for once in your life?' She raises her hand like she's going to slap my face but a policeman steps between us.

I open my mouth to tell her but nothing comes out except a groan.

CHAPTER 10
The Worst Day

Douggie

Listen. Hear them whispering, telling lies? They say I've done something wrong, something bad. Too bad to be real. The pigs have been at me for hours, making threats, asking questions till I don't know if my dick's my own. Not sure what happened in the first place. But things aren't looking good. They've locked me in here and it stinks of ancient piss. This isn't how a star should be treated. Didn't Paris get a room of her own? Didn't she get a TV?

There's no sound but their whispering, telling lies about what they say I've done. But how could I have done it? Was I even there?

What if I did?

I bang my head against the bars of the cell till my eyebrow splits and blood mixes with the tears and snot on my cheeks. I keep banging till they give me a pill of something that makes me feel as if I've floated away from my body. Like I'm someone else. The old me, before things went to shit and everyone got jealous.

Lying down on the bunk, I curl up in the scratchy blanket that reeks of old-man sweat and wedge my hands between my thighs. Take myself somewhere else, somewhere good.

It's weird what pops into my head. I mean I haven't thought about primary school forever, and here I am in lock-up thinking about that day about a year after Dad died when Beck and I were forced to dance together in front of the whole of grade seven. I used to think it was the worst day of my life.

Beck was paying out on me as usual. 'Think you're pretty cool, don't you? With your long hair and smoking behind the shed and everything. Well you're not, Douglas Spencer. You're stupid. Just a stupid kid like the rest of us. So shut up and dance.'

I got her back. I called her Cock-a-roach, because her last name's Roche. She was a goody-goody and a dag in those days, and worst of all, she was Russ's sister and lived just three doors down from our place, so there was no avoiding her. Even on the weekends.

Me and Steve used to sit together up the back of the classroom, but a couple of weeks earlier Miss Bateman had moved me right up the front with freckle-head blood-nut Rebecca, and made Steve sit next to Ronald Forrester, a brain with thick glasses. Miss wanted to have us close, she said, to keep an eye on us. Sometimes she leant right over me so I saw every wrinkle on her old lady face and smelt the eggs she'd had for breakfast.

I hated sitting next to Beck and drew rude pictures of her with a dog's face covered in spots which I folded into paper planes and flew over to Steve when Miss wasn't looking. Steve almost wet his pants, he thought it was so funny. It was cool being seniors together. Bosses of the whole school. The little kids did anything we said, gave us their iceblocks or lollies whenever we asked. It was like being a king. It was good to be kings at school, when we were grommets on the weekends with Brian and the gang.

But right then I had to hold Beck's hands and do the stupid Pride of Erin in front of everyone. They were lined up around the edges of the bitumen parade ground, watching and laughing. I don't know why Miss picked me to do it. I wasn't the best dancer in those days. It's taken a while to learn the moves I've got now.

Up, two, three, kick. Back, two, three, kick. Beck kicked before me and made a face when I swung her around. Over her shoulder I caught a glimpse of Steve. He gave me a look of sympathy but he couldn't cover up the grin that told the truth. I looked like a total dickhead.

It wasn't fair. Why hadn't Miss picked him? My hands were sweaty and Beck was looking down her nose at me as usual. Even worse, I was going to be covered in girls' germs, Cock-a-roach germs! I could've died. Man, if only I knew then what I know now. Give me girl germs, I want to swim in them.

We were practising some dances for our 'passing out' night at the end of the year. I didn't even want to go. But it turned out kind of cool after me and Steve scabbed a joint and some beer off Brian before we went. That made it fun all right. I've always liked smoking joints, makes everything a bit magic. Things look better, colours are brighter, lollies taste sweeter, jokes are funnier. It's sort of like changing from black and white TV to colour.

Right from when I got up that morning I knew it was going to be a freaky kind of day. Mum was sitting on my bed wild-eyed and excited about something. I don't think she'd been to sleep all night long. It'd been less than a year since Dad died and she was still freaking right out. She smelt like vodka and cigarettes, her curly brown hair was messed up and her face looked like the skin was stretched too tight across the bones. She used to be pretty, my Mum. You should see her in some of the photos, like the wedding one. She looks beautiful in that. Got my looks from her I guess. Though my nose is better than hers, and my cheekbones are higher.

'Time to get up now, darling,' she said, then started singing some kooky old-fashioned song. 'Wake up, wake up, wake up you sleepy head. Get up, get up, get up, get out of bed, lala, la, la la.' She didn't know all the words but it still sounded good to hear her sing. She used to sing to me all the time when I was little, but ever since Dad died she only sang once in a blue moon, and it was usually some sad old song about a broken heart.

'Guess what?' she said, like she had some wonderful surprise.

'What?' I asked, picking yesterday's school shirt off the floor and tugging it over my head.

'I'm going to walk with you to school this morning. It's about time I introduced myself to your teacher.'

Some great surprise.

'You don't have to Mum, you look tired. Why don't you go to bed?' I said, trying to get out of it.

'Oh, no. I'm not tired. I feel like today's the beginning of something wonderful for all of us. You just wait and see, Douggie. Mummy's going to get her act together and be a proper mother from now on.'

'But you are a proper mum,' I told her and it's still true. She may not be the same as she was before Dad died, but she's still my mum and I love her, even when she forgets to make dinner and falls asleep in front of the telly with a cigarette in her hand. She's just sad, that's all.

She covered me in big sloppy kisses after I said that, even though I was thirteen, too big for kissing. I tried to wriggle away but not too hard. It felt kind of nice to have a cuddle.

Brian was already up and eating toast in the kitchen. He nodded in my direction as I came in scratching my head and pulling on my shorts. I couldn't find any undies in my drawers.

'What's up with Mum today?' I asked.

'Buggered if I know.'

I rummaged in the bread bin.

'Last piece.' Brian waved the last bite of Vegemite toast in the air before shoving it in his mouth.

'There's no bread left, Mum,' I said as she came in. She'd got dressed and put on makeup, orange stripes on her cheeks and shiny blue eyeshadow so she looked like the cover of the Women's Weekly.

'No problem, I'll make pancakes instead,' she said and started bustling around, crashing things in the cupboards.

'I'm off,' said Brian. 'I'm meeting Jacko down the park to have a kick before school.' But he wasn't. They were pulling cones instead.

'Can I come?'

'No way, no grommets allowed. Maybe on the weekend,' he said over his shoulder as he slammed the screen door behind him.

I thought Brian was the coolest big brother in the world then. Everyone wanted to be like him and Jacko, not just me. On the weekends we had some wild times. Sure they called us grommets and paid out on us big time but it was cool to smoke joints and drink goon with them. Besides, what else was I supposed to do?

Mum tipped flour into a bowl to make pancakes.

'Can I help?' I asked.

'Sure. Get out some milk and eggs, would you?'

When I was really little, Mum used to let me help her make cakes all the time. We used to do lots of stuff together. I still remember.

But there weren't any eggs, or much milk either.

Mum and I had glue biscuits with jam for breakfast. We both pretended they were delicious.

By the time I looked at the clock it was almost nine, so I was happy when Mum offered to drive me to school. I should've just made a run for it. Mum screeched out of the driveway at a hundred miles an hour, almost killed three kids and an old lady who were crossing the road, and jumped the gutter in front of school.

'Thanks Mum,' I said, already half out the door. 'See ya.'

'Wait for me. I'm coming to meet your teacher, remember?'

How could I forget?

'You don't need to. Really. She doesn't like to meet parents.'

'Oh don't be silly. I'm coming and that's that.'

Luckily the bell had gone and almost everyone was already in their classrooms, so I didn't have the horror of an oval full of kids seeing me walk in holding my Mum's hand. I tried not to but she kept grasping for it, so I had to.

At least she looked okay. She was wearing a pretty dress with flowers on it. But the straps kept falling down so you could see her bra, and she was still wearing her slippers.

'You've got your slippers on,' I whispered as we walked up the stairs to the top floor. I could hear Miss Bateman calling the roll in her posh voice.

'Oops,' Mum giggled looking down at her pink scuffs. 'Don't worry. She won't even notice.'

But I knew better. 'Maybe you should see her another day.'

Too late. We were at the door and Miss was looking over her cats-eye glasses at us from behind her desk. She seemed kind of surprised. I watched as her eyes moved over my mother, straight to her feet.

Her eyebrows moved up but at least she didn't say anything except, 'Can I help you?'

Mum went to say something but the words got stuck in her throat so I said, 'It's my mum, Miss Bateman. She wants to say hello.'

As Miss came walking over, smoothing her long skirt, I rushed to my desk, trying not to look, praying Mum wouldn't find out how often I'd been up the office lately and that she wouldn't say anything too embarrassing.

'Nice slippers,' said Beck with a smirk.

'Shut up.'

I rummaged in my desk for books, determined not to look around. But I knew, even without seeing it, that the whole class was giggling and whispering and watching every move my mother made. My ears felt sunburnt they were that hot.

Then, just as I thought it couldn't possibly get any worse, it did. Miss went back to the front of the room and Mum came trailing behind her, heading straight for my desk.

She's not going to... No! Oh God please no! I felt like I was waist deep in creek mud, sinking deeper with every step she took towards me. In my imagination only my head was still out when it happened. She gave me a big kiss, right in front of everyone.

Plop! My whole head went under; so that Steve's guffaws and Beck's high pitched giggles were muffled. I kept my eyes screwed up tight till I couldn't hear anything except the shuffle of Mum's slippers moving away and the door closing behind her. Miss Bateman's voice droned on and on. Right then I never wanted her to stop talking.

You'd think that was enough embarrassment for one day, but no. It was like God was having a pick-on-Douggie day, just for laughs. It was really hot at lunchtime so, after sharing a ciggie down behind the swimming shed, Steve and I started a water fight, ballooning our cheeks with water from the taps and spitting it over Gary and Tim.

Other kids joined in and we were having a great time chasing each other around the school, squirting and bucketing each other. We were laughing and concentrating on filling up bottles when Gary and Tim came up behind us and pulled down our shorts all the way to our ankles.

Dakked!

Suddenly kids were everywhere as we scrambled to pull up our pants. It was okay for Steve, at least he had undies, but I didn't have any.

The whole world saw my bum. And then I swear I heard someone say, 'Check out Doug Spencer's willy! It's as big as a Twistie!'

I hitched up my daks and roared after Tim, my eyes firmly on his stubbies, when I bolted around the corner and crashed straight into Mr Heggy, the headmaster.

He grabbed me by the ear. 'Just what do you think you're up to, young man?'

'Tim dakked me, Sir.'

'Look at the state of you. The bell's about to go. Go to the sick room and get a towel to dry off. You too Steve. I've got my eye on you boys; I don't want to see you in my office again this month. Got it?'

'Yes sir.'

So there I was, still slightly damp, standing in front of a class who had all seen my willy and watched my mother kiss me. And to top it all off, I had my arms around Beck Roche, the biggest goody-goody dag in the whole Universe, dancing.

'No Douggie, like this,' hissed Beck, grabbing my hand and pulling me to where she wanted me.

'This way?'

'No. Put one arm here and hold my hand. Okay, now spin us around a bit.'

So I did. Steve was pissing himself. But I wasn't looking at him anymore. I looked at my feet, making sure I didn't mess up. I could do without falling over in front of everyone.

'You're doing very well, Douglas,' said Miss Bateman. 'Now just look up. No, not that far. Just at Beck. That's right.'

I looked at Beck and, so I didn't have to stare at her eyes, I started counting her freckles. She had lots of them, not big ones like some kids, millions of tiny freckles like a fairy bread sandwich.

'Your freckles are like hundreds and thousands,' I said without thinking.

'Thanks,' she said, and smiled, like it was something good to say.

She shouldn't have smiled; I wouldn't have liked it if someone called me a freckle-head. But she didn't seem to mind.

It was time for the rest of the class to dance as well, so we stopped spinning and got ready to start again with the one two three stuff.

When the music began, me and Beck were the first to go forward, bumping into the back of Steve and Susan Lock, who was two times as tall as him and three times as narrow. They were still figuring out how to hold hands.

Beck and I looked at each other and raised our eyebrows.

'Losers,' whispered Beck, and I laughed.

By the time we got up to the waltzing bit again I knew that Beck's eyes were green, with a little bit of grey, and that she liked fishing as much as I did.

We were talking so much as we twirled around that we didn't even notice that the music had stopped and Miss was clapping her hands to make everyone shut up.

'Douglas and Rebecca,' she said, but she didn't sound angry.

Everyone was looking at us, so we dropped hands and quickly moved away from each other, got into our lines and paraded back up the stairs.

As we settled back into our chairs, Beck said, 'I didn't mean it, you know.'

'What?'

'About you being stupid.'

'That's okay. You're not too stupid either.'

'And I'm sorry I teased you about your mum,' she said in a rush like she had to get it out fast.

'I suppose she is a bit weird.'

'All mums are weird. You should see mine,' she said, pointing her finger and making the coo-coo sign around her ear.

I smiled at her and I didn't even care if Steve saw.

It wasn't such a bad day. I'd do anything to have it back again. To start right there and do everything different. But it's too late. Everything's gone wrong. I'm in the fucking lock up and Beck's with Jacko getting wasted every day, rooting a bastard like that when she should be with me. Wish I had a magic raft to ride back in time with the current. It should've been me and her. We'd have been good together. There's still a chance I reckon. Once Jacko's out of the picture. He never stays with a girl for long.

But I've got to sort this shit of a mess out first. Got to get out of here.

It can't be true what they're saying about me. Must be one of their plots. All of them against me, trying to keep the women for themselves. Get rid of me. Get rid of me for good, if what the pigs are saying I've done is true. I can't think about it now. Can't let that night come back into my head. I'm just going to lie here and think about Beck, about me and her together. Maybe I'll write her a song. Yeah, that's it. That'll have her begging for it, just like all the other chicks.

Tell you what though. I'm never taking bloody acid again.

CHAPTER 11

Bloody Virgin

Beck

Pop. More a feeling than a sound. Something breaking. At last. Jacko's inside me.

He didn't want to do it, happy with another head job, but I talked him into it.

'I'm ready,' I said, fed up with being the only sixteen-year-old virgin left in Brisbane. We could've done it before, there've been lots of other nights, but I wanted it to be special. Wait for the right time. The right night. The right boy. Jacko. An act of love to tie us together, keep him close to me when everything else is falling apart.

Now at last the moment has come.

Into the darkness and the smell of rum where his face should be, I whisper the words I've been practising for half a year.

'I love you.'

He raises himself up, straightening his arms. 'Fuck. What did you have to go and say that for?' he says. 'I don't love you. What the fuck's that supposed to mean?'

His words pin me to the bed.

'Why'd you have to go and ruin everything? I've had enough of your bullshit. All the pathetic moaning and crying over Russ. Get over it for fuck's sake. That was months ago. Why don't you go out with one of the other fellas? Brian really needs a root. Or what about Steve? Shit even Douggie reckons you're okay.' He prises himself out of me and flops onto his back in the narrow bed. 'I knew it was a mistake not to piss you off sooner. And this is what feeling sorry for someone gets me? Virgins. I should've known better.' He rolls over and faces the wall.

I lie stiff, holding myself away from him, trying to swallow the hurt that's stuck in the back of my throat.

'But,' I say, 'but...'

'But I've been sharing your bed every weekend,' I want to say. 'You've been kissing me, holding me. How can you not love me? What's all this been if it hasn't been love?'

He falls asleep snoring, open-mouthed. The stink of rum seeps from his pores, and mine. The smell of his sweat is on my skin. How can I have been so wrong? I've been saving myself for my 'true love', the 'one'. The way you're supposed to. I thought he was it.

Of course he's never said he loves me, though I've thought I've seen it in his eyes. Haven't I? We've been hanging out for ages. I thought he was my boyfriend. Sure we don't spend much daylight time together.

But the nights, especially since Russ drowned and I practically moved into his place to get away from the misery of home, the nights we spend wrapped in each other's arms, breathing the same breath. Isn't that love? Or am I just a pity-fuck? Not a choice he's made. Are all the grand love stories and romantic dreams only in my head? An alcohol-soaked delusion? Idiot.

When I wake up, foul-mouthed and bleary in the morning, he's gone. I'm glad. What could I say? How could I look at that face I once thought so beautiful, knowing that he could flick me away without feeling a thing except perhaps relief?

I grab my t-shirt from the floor and pull it over my head. It reeks of the rum I spilt down the front and all the cigarettes and bongs I smoked. As I stand up something gushes between my thighs. Blood.

Leaving a trail of splatters on the carpet I hobble cross-legged to the bathroom. Thank God it's a weekday and the house is empty. It's been pretty dismal around here since Russ died. Jacko acts like nothing's changed, but it has. And then Douggie did what he did. Kids are spooked. There's a brittle edge to the laughter at parties, as if everyone's scared that as soon as they stop laughing they'll cry. Like me.

Though this morning under the shower I can't help smiling a little to myself as the rose-coloured water swirls down the drain. Maybe it doesn't matter so much that he doesn't love me. I've done it. I'm not a virgin anymore. Now I'm a real woman, just like a Jewish bride on bloodied sheets. I am 'deflowered'. A maiden no longer, or whatever shit they say in those old books.

I clean myself up, put on a pad and scrub at the stains on the carpet, the detergent foam turning pink. But when I go to the toilet a short time later the pad is already overflowing scarlet. I put on another one but soon it too is thick and heavy with blood. I change it again and again as I sit staring at daytime T.V. hoping it will just go away.

I know something is wrong. I'm sure it's not supposed to be like this. I read a story once about a girl who'd almost bled to death after her first time. I thought it was ridiculous, a horror story to put girls off sex. Now I realise it just might have been true.

I ring Pete, he knows more about sex than any woman, and tell him what's happened. I don't tell him what I said to Jacko in the dark and his awful reply. That hurts more than the weeping wound between my legs.

Pete leaves work and comes over. When he sees me he insists on taking me down the road to the doctor. I don't see the need. Do I look that bad? I stare at my pale face in the mirror. Surely the bleeding will stop by itself. It doesn't hurt much, I just feel a bit tired that's all. But I have to get some more pads from the shops anyway, so I let Pete talk me into it.

I lean heavy on his shoulder as we walk the five hundred metres to the doctor's surgery. The road stretches and shimmers in the summer heat, the pad sticky in my pants. We sit in the waiting room of the family G.P. waiting and whispering, flicking through old women's magazines, staring at faded health posters. I'm anxious. The pad is full and needs changing. Soon it will leak, all over my skirt and the chair and I'll have to deal with that shame as well.

Eventually the doctor's receptionist beckons me into the office.

The doctor looks like he's wearing a Groucho Marx mask, all nose, moustache and black horn-rimmed glasses. He even smells of cigars. He scrambles through the piles of paper and medical samples on his desk for my file, a page of yellowing foolscap filled with scribbled notes about asthma aggravated by smoking, antibiotics to fight chest infections, sedatives and a course of anti-depressants.

'What seems to be the trouble this time?' he asks.

'I had sex for the first time last night and something's wrong. I'm bleeding.'

'Bleeding. Well that's quite usual.'

'It's a lot. I'm bleeding a lot.'

'Well that should stop soon enough.'

'I don't think so; it seems to be getting worse.'

He sighs and puts down his pen.

'I suppose I'd better have a look at you then. Get up on the table.' Stretching on some gloves, he nods in the direction of the narrow examination table against the wall decorated with peeling transfers of Winnie the Pooh.

'Pull up your skirt. Get rid of your pants. Open your legs.' He says with his back to me. He turns around and I hear him swallow.

'For goodness sake, young lady. What on earth have you done to yourself? What a mess.'

'It was just sex. Just me and my... my boyfriend. Sex, that's all. Normal. My first time.'

He fumbles around with his plastic coated hands, hurting, poking, prodding.

'There's nothing I can do here,' he says, 'you'll have to go to hospital and get stitched up. Pull up your pants and get down. I've finished with you.'

He tut tuts. 'Just look at the mess you've made of my table.'

His neat white bed is smeared with scarlet and plum jam blood clots, his white gloves stained red as he peels them into the sink. He writes a referral and hurries me out of the room, calling for the receptionist to come and clean up the mess.

'You get yourself to the hospital right now,' he says, 'or you could bleed to death.'

He glowers at Pete who stands up as I come out. 'What have you got to say for yourself young man?'

Pete laughs and puts his arm around me.

'It wasn't him,' I whisper.

We go to the hospital in a taxi and soon I'm on a trolley in a gown and cap, pale and frightened, being wheeled down corridors stinking of disinfectant. I have to let Pete's hand go as they push me into surgery. My legs are strapped into stirrups and a nurse looks down at me with pity as the surgeon stitches my hymen back together again.

A virgin remade.

All that trouble for nothing.

Later the gynaecologist explains. My hymen was like a shield of steel, thick and hard, impenetrable. No wonder I always found tampons unwearable, hobbling along spread-legged with half the tampon dangling between my thighs. Do the gods mean for me to be a nun? Is this some kind of a sign? Or a punishment.

That night in the crowded ward full of middle-aged women nursing fresh hysterectomy stitches, I lie awake trying to understand what's happened. I decide to take the steel from my hymen and wrap it, tight, around my heart. I'm not going to cry over Jacko. I'm not going to cry over any boy, except my brother, ever. I won't open my door to Jacko again. My shield of steel will protect me. I'll forget him, lock him out of my life, and never look back.

When Mum drives me back home the next morning there's a sorry looking bunch of supermarket flowers in cellophane lying on the front step.

I step over them and go inside, closing the door behind me.

CHAPTER 12
Hunting

Douggie

So you want to know what happened? What I did?

The acid had been around for months but bloody Brian never let me do any, even though he was taking a tab every weekend. I wasn't allowed, he said, not after all the loony stuff. But I'd been taking my pills.

'I'm fine,' I told him. 'I can handle it. I can hold my booze and my smoke as well as you can. I deserve to have a go. Just because you reckon I'm schizo is no reason for me to miss out on all the fun.' I was sick of being left out. It wasn't fair. Everyone reckoned acid was unreal, totally wild. I was dying to try some.

Tables and Chairs they were called. Little blue cardboard squares with pink pictures in the middle. Didn't look much like furniture.

'Pure. Real fucken sweet. Good shit,' said the guy who was handing them around at the party, stuffing money into his jeans pockets.

I had my cash ready this time, and shoved my crumpled notes into the dude's hand before Brian had a chance to stop me.

But as usual he had to cramp my style. 'No way,' he said, 'He's on drugs.'

'Aren't we all mate, aren't we all?' The guy dropped one into my hand before Brian had a chance to stammer, 'No man, not like that. He's schizo.'

I chucked it into my mouth and swallowed.

'Oops,' said the dealer.

'Too late now, Brian,' I skited, patting my belly.

He rolled his eyes and shrugged. 'Don't go blaming me when you freak out. I'm not going to baby you if you can't hack the pace. You'd better not spoil my trip.'

'I'm not going to freak. I can handle it. I had more mushies than you that time you ended up on the roof talking to God.'

'Shut up about that. Do what you like. Just don't come crawling to me later.' He put a tab in his mouth and left the circle.

'You going to be all right, Douggie?' asked Steve, sucking on his own square of acid.

'Yeah sure. Why shouldn't I be? You fellas are a bunch of old women.'

'Anyway, I'll keep an eye on you.'

'Thanks mate. I'll watch your back too.'

'What's up with Jacko tonight?' Steve asked. We looked over to where Jacko was sitting on the couch pulling cones one after the other. Beck was pressed to his side as usual. It looked like she'd been crying over Russ again.

'They had a fight or something. He was yelling at her before.'

'Women.'

'Oh come on, Beck's all right. Jacko can be a real arsehole sometimes. Doesn't know how to treat a woman like I do.'

'Yeah right, Douggie the Sex God. Don't get started.'

Everyone was in the lounge room, some at the table by the window with Jacko and Beck, pulling cones in the skull bong, playing cards and drinking rum from the bottle. The rest were hanging around the couch where the bucket bong was in action, some poor fella coughing his guts out like he was going to cark it. Steve and me squashed in together on one of the couch's red vinyl arms and waited our turn. A tidemark of black slime and green specks was smeared half way up the cut off plastic bottle that was slowly being pulled out of the water and filling with smoke. It smelt good, familiar. Safe.

The telly was on but with the sound down. The zombies on the screen seemed to be marching in time to the AC/DC on the stereo. A whole pile of other DVDs with bloody covers were on the floor for later. Jacko loves horror shows.

There were a few girls hanging around. Beck, but she was glued to Jacko's side and off limits. Her friend, Angie, but she was with that big Goth, Jase. There were a few new faces too, not bad some of them, though they were all sucking up to that poofter Pete.

But anyway, tonight was for the fellas. A tripping party. Men together, off our faces. It was a special night. I could feel it. The trip in my guts was my chance to prove that I wasn't a fucking mad bastard anymore. I was just like all of them. One of the gang again.

Half an hour later, Steve and I were rolling on the floor, pissing ourselves. We'd had a couple of buckets, but when I looked at the cigarette burns in the floral carpet and they started to swirl and go all psychedelic like an album cover, I knew I was tripping.

'Hey Steve, I think it's happening.'

'Yeah man. Check out the curtains.'

We laughed and spun around in circles till everything was a crazy mixed up whirl, like a rainbow cake mix. In the bottom of the kitchen cupboard we found the tinfoil and made ourselves space hats and ran around the house pretending to zap each other. Jacko got pissed off with us making too much noise and getting in the way of the

TV, so he shoved us out into the front yard and told me to shut up or they wouldn't let me back in.

It was great outside. The stars were like sparklers and when the Taubmans' paint factory sign came on across the road in red and blue, it was like an outer space sunset or something. The most beautiful thing I've ever seen.

Then my head started to go really weird on me. All the colours got too much. I couldn't see the real shape of things anymore and Steve's face seemed to be melting. He changed into one of those freaky zombies. Barking dogs' heads were sprouting from my legs. The grass was too pointy under my feet. My tongue felt swollen. Too big for my mouth.

I started to pull at it, but it didn't feel like my tongue anymore, not a part of me. An alien or zombie or something had possessed me and turned into a huge slimy slug growing in my mouth. I tugged at it and clawed but I couldn't get it out. Steve tried to stop me but I punched him away. Or was it him? I screamed.

Steve came back with Brian who grabbed my arms, pinned them behind my back, pushed me into the house and onto the couch and shouted at me, 'Just stay there, and don't do anything else stupid. I told you you'd freak out. Shit.' And then went back to the table to pull cones.

Steve sat next to me but I didn't want him to. Well I did but I didn't. I was scared to be by myself but I knew I couldn't trust him. It was like I could see inside people to what they really were, slugs or zombies. Monsters. I tried to focus, keep my head from turning itself inside out, by staring at the TV, though I couldn't see a picture – only the red and blue and yellow dots behind it.

Brian and a few of the other fellas were still sucking bucket bongs.

'Let's go dancing!' yelled one of the girls.

'Nah, we're too out of it. They'd never let us in,' said Jacko.

So they started dancing in the lounge room. They pushed back the couch with me and Steve huddling wide eyed in a corner of it, cleared a space and put on some rap, then started throwing themselves against walls, making the house shake.

I couldn't move. I just sat staring at the jumping legs and waving arms, watching as the dancers morphed into creatures from galaxies far away.

———

Next thing I knew someone was sprinkling me with salt and sticking a fork into my arm.

'Hey!'

'We're hungry.'

That snapped me out of it. 'Shit!' I got up quick smart. 'Get away from me, Jacko. Where's Brian? Bri!'

'Come on, Jacko. Leave Douggie alone. He was freaking before,' said Beck. Always knew she had a soft spot for me, that kiss did the trick.

'So? Who the fuck asked you?' said Jacko, but he stopped jabbing me with the fork.

Where was Brian? Maybe the aliens got him.

'Come on, let's go out,' said Jacko, 'I'm going bloody stir-crazy in here. Let's go do something.'

'What?' everyone yelled over the music.

'I dunno. Anything. We'll make it up as we go along. Everyone bring something.'

The fellas rattled around collecting stuff to take, buckets and bike chains and power tools and saucepans. Steve shoved a kitchen knife into my hand. 'Here. In case he tries to eat you again.' He was holding a potato masher.

I didn't want to go anywhere. Everyone was acting wild, whooping and calling, waving knives and chains and hammers around their heads. Playing war games. I just wanted to stay sitting on the couch with Steve, trying to watch TV, maybe make my move on Beck once I could think a bit straighter.

Through the crack in the door I spied Brian in Jacko's room with his arm around Beck, who was sobbing again. He was edging his hand up under the back of her t-shirt, trying to cop a feel. Bloody hell. As if she'd look at Brian when I was around. He obviously wasn't thinking about what Jacko would do if he caught him either.

'I don't want any part of it,' said Jase, packing another cone and passing it to Pete.

'Loser,' said Jacko, as he pushed me and Steve into the parade that was already starting out the backdoor. 'Come on you dickheads. We're going hunting.'

It was cold outside. Cold and wet like it was raining a bit, ticklish on my skin. I wished I could take some of that soft rain and scrub it around inside my head where all the monsters were hiding.

We climbed over the fence and stumbled through the neighbour's yard to the road.

'Where're we going?' I whispered to Steve.

'Dunno. Just hunting I guess.'

'I'm hungry,' said Jacko, 'bloody starving.'

'Me too,' said some of the other guys.

'Me too,' we echoed.

A possum scuttled across a nearby roof, its claws scratching on the tin.

'Meat!' Jacko roared.

And we hunters stampeded in the direction of the sound. Not that any of us had ever eaten possum or knew how to skin one or anything. But it seemed like a good idea.

'Meat! Meat! Meat!' we all chanted, like we were cave men hunting T-Rex. It felt great. Hunting together. I was glad Jacko made me come. It chased away the spooks from my brain, cleared it with the cry of 'Meat! Meat! Meat!'

Something scurried behind a bin out on the footpath.

'There it is!'

'Get it!'

'Get it Jacko.'

'Kill it!' we screamed.

We threw the bins over and Jacko swung down his chain with a heavy thunk onto the shadow.

It wasn't a possum.

He picked it up, limp and sagging, and we saw that it was a cat, a fat old cat with its brains smashed in. Jacko took it by the tail and spun it around his head like a lasso, whooping and pounding his chest with his other hand.

That started us all doing an Indian war dance, making 'Wa, wa, wa, wa,' noises with our hands slapping on our mouths, just like they do on TV, dancing around Jacko and the cat.

A light came on at a window so we raced down the road laughing and hollering till we got to the park. Jacko threw the cat up into a tree where it stuck in the branches. He wiped the blood from his hands across his cheeks like war paint.

'I know,' he said. 'Let's do a job, get some money and go into town. Get some burgers at that all-night takeaway.'

'Yeah, yeah.' We all thought it was a brilliant idea. It would be a piece of piss.

At the edge of the park there was a rich looking sort of a house, brick with rose bushes and those big fluffy flowers on real long stems. A window was open. A small one. Up high.

'Get here Douggie,' ordered Jacko.

And I was pushed forward. I didn't want to go. But I wanted Jacko and the fellas to like me again, to show them I was good for something. That it paid to keep me around.

Up on top of Jacko's shoulders everything started spinning and going weird, the window seemed way too small, like I was Alice in that story where she filled up a whole house.

'I'm not gunna fit,' I whispered down to him.

'Course you can. Don't pike on us now. Just get in and open the door. We'll do the rest.'

'It's too small,' I whimpered.

'Fuck you, Loony. Just do it,' said Jacko pushing hard on my bum till I fell through, half on a toilet, half on cold tiles. My knife clattered into the bathtub beside me.

'I'm in!' I yelled.

'Shut up, you dickwad,' came the hiss back. 'Just let us in.'

It was dark. And quiet. I picked up my knife and followed the moonlight on the blade deeper into the house. Inside it smelt like disinfectant and furniture polish and like something good had been cooked for tea. I was hungry. It'd been a long time since lunch the day before.

I found the kitchen. The fridge shone white like a space-age treasure chest. Inside, it was full of good things to eat, the sort of things you always wish you'd find when you get home from school starving. Cakes and chocolate milk and custard and pies and chicken.

There was a whole big plate full of what looked like Kentucky Fried, and even some roast potatoes. I couldn't believe my luck. I propped the door open with my body, tucked my knife into the top of my jeans and shoveled in chicken and potatoes, scooped out hunks of apricot pie with my fist. In my mouth it turned real weird, more like sponges than food. I gagged.

The overhead fluorescent light flashed on. Flicker. Flicker. BANG! I was blinded.

Something was coming towards me. Something big and mean and ugly. I grabbed my knife and lashed out. It was a trap. An alien blood-sucking trap. They'd all been in on it.

My hands were slippery with chicken and pie but when I held them both around the handle of my knife I got a good grip. I swung and moved forward, scrunching my eyes closed. Swung again.

Hit something.

A cry. A cat. Meeeeooooow.

I peeked and caught a glimpse. A giant white cat, an alien cat with lumpy pink bits instead of ears.

I aimed and lunged. Got it!

Screech.

Laughing, I swung again. It felt good, like I was strong. Invincible. Like it was connecting me to the earth and to all hunters, to the cave men. Like I was part of some great cosmic plan.

Something heavy fell, hit the table, and thudded onto the lino. I squeezed my eyes tight trying to get a picture, flick onto the right channel. The thing moved so I lunged towards it again.

The rattling and banging at the door made me stop. Then I remembered. The fellas. Wait till they saw what I'd done. Douggie the alien killer. They'd carry me on their shoulders, cheer, go crazy. I'd be a hero, a king.

'What took you so long?' came Jacko's voice through the door as my hands slipped on the doorknob. 'Why'd you turn the light on?'

Still smiling I opened the door and the boys came pouring in bringing the dark night with them.

'What were you doing, Douggie?'

Then they saw it.

Her.

The old lady.

She was lying curled up beside the table in a white nightie, her hair in fat pink curlers. Her hands were up in front of her face and there were slashes like claw marks on her arms. The alien must've got her.

Jacko was the first back out the door.

'What've you done? You fucking crazy cunt. What the fuck have you done?'

Words of Love

Brian

After they locked Douggie away, Jacko finally broke up with Beck. As part of his celebrations, he'd decided we needed to grow our own dope, so he dug up a circle of lawn in the backyard with his new motorbike, doing spin outs, chunks of turf and dirt flying everywhere, laughing like a maniac. Then he shaved off the eyebrows of some young fellas, so there were a whole lot of grommets running around looking like freaky lizard-people. They thought they looked cool, that it meant Jacko liked them. Maybe it did.

One night a few weeks after that, I woke up with Jacko leaning over me, shaking me by the shoulders.

'Brian! Wake up man. Ya gotta help me. It's all falling apart.'

I put my hands up to my forehead to check that my eyebrows were still there, then peeled his hands off me. His eyes were wild. He'd shaved off the hair above the ears on both sides of his head.

'What's up with your hair, mate?' I laughed, trying to calm him down, but he was jumping around my room like his feet were on fire.

'Fuck man! Get up! Everything's about to go. We gotta get out of here!'

'What? You're just tripping mate, freaking out. Take a valium.' But he wasn't listening. He started banging his fists so hard into his forehead I thought he was going to make a hole.

I knew I wasn't going to be able to roll over and go back to sleep. He was freaking out big time. So I got up, grabbed his arms, and made him sit down next to me on the bed.

'Brian? It's really you isn't it?' His eyes had that same spaced-out look Douggie's had had when he first flipped out. My guts leapt into my mouth. Not Jacko too. I couldn't stand it. I've had enough of crazy.

'It's me. Just calm down. It's the acid that's all. Let's go get a bit of fresh air.' Seeing the moon and trees and stuff usually calmed people down.

'It's all falling apart,' he whispered. 'Man, everything's gone evil.'

'Forget about it.' I put my arm around his shoulders and led him out the back. We sat on the stairs and I showed him the stars and how everything was just the same, how it wasn't falling down. Sort of patting him a bit.

He stopped panicking after a while and leant over, resting his head on me.

'Thanks,' he said. 'You're a real mate. You really are.'

'Yeah, yeah. I love you too.' And I did. We'd been best friends for years, been through all sorts of shit together. He knew me better than anyone. And I knew him. At least I thought I did. 'Don't worry mate. Everything's okay. You just did too much acid tonight, that's all,' I said.

He nodded, still with his head nestled into me like I was his mother. And I sat there with my arm around him on the stairs, looking out at the moon, thinking.

And then a few weeks later I found them: all tangled together on top of the bare mattress, the sheets in a pile on the floor. They didn't even grab for the covers when they saw me. Jacko looked up as if it was nothing, as if it was just another girl I'd found him with.

I guess I should have knocked.

I should never have let those Goths into the house. They seemed harmless enough, once you got over their stupid haircuts and clothes. And I really didn't have a choice once they started coming in with Beck. When Jacko dropped her, I thought that'd be the end of it, but that bloody Pete kept turning up like an odd sock.

'Bums to the wall!' we'd joke when we saw him coming up the drive in his pointy boots and flouncy shirts. But he was all right. He'd have a laugh with us and wasn't too girly. If it weren't for his makeup and some of the things he said, you'd never have known. And Jacko liked him. Started getting into the music he brought over, even though I thought it was garbage. Some nights he'd sit next to Pete for hours and they'd natter away like two old ladies, talking about music and drugs and shit. I'd give up trying to get a word in, and go to bed to have a private joint and wank over some porno.

The house just wasn't what it used to be. No Russ. Douggie locked up. And then the bloody Goths. They changed it somehow. Changed Jacko. He'd rather talk to Pete than have a drink with me.

I suppose I should've noticed something, but I never saw them touching, no holding hands or stuff like that. Once I thought I saw them smiling at each other across the room over something they found funny but no one else did. A private joke. Jacko started showering more often. That should've told me something was up, but I just thought he was finally getting my hints.

I suppose there were signs, but I didn't think it was possible. Not Jacko. We were best mates, I'd have known something like that about him. He'd have told me. We'd done everything together till that Pete came along. Shared bongs, girls, shared life really. I'd seen a different girl come out of his room every night since he'd broken up with Beck.

That's why I didn't knock.

'Gidday,' Jacko said like it was any other morning. 'Wild party hey?'

'Morning,' said Pete. 'Got a hangover or what? I was totally wasted.'

'I, ah... sorry,' I said and backed out quick smart, feeling as if I was about to fall down. They'd had their arms, their hands, all over each other, like they couldn't let go. I stumbled like a blind man across to the bong table where Steve and a few of the others were pulling the first cones of the morning.

'Fuck man, what's up with you? You look like shit,' said Steve, through a steady stream of smoke.

I couldn't tell him. I couldn't tell anyone. I shook my head to try and clear the image of hairy legs rubbing together, and stuck my hands out for the bong. 'Nothing a cone or two won't fix,' I said and hoped to God that everyone would clear off in a hurry so that no one would ever know but me.

But ten minutes later Jacko and Pete waltzed out of the bedroom and headed straight over, arms draped around each other like newlyweds. Then Pete sat on Jacko's lap. Right there, in front of everyone. Jacko wrapped his arms around Pete's waist, puffed up his chest and stuck out his chin, daring me to say anything.

'I'll pack cones,' said Pete, like he owned the place.

I felt like crying. Don't know why. It felt like I'd lost something, worse than losing a dope deal with no money to buy more. It felt like Jacko and I would never be the same, that I could never be best mates with him again. So I pushed back my chair and left without a word. The others sat there open-mouthed as Jacko took up his usual position as commander of the bong, passing the mull-bowl to Pete. It was Jacko's dope. What did they care who sat on his lap?

I got out of the house as fast as I could. Walked down to the river and kept going. Walked all the way back to Mum's. We went to the loony bin and hung out with Douggie for a while. Didn't tell him about Jacko though, didn't know what to say. Besides, Mum was there. By the time we got back to Mum's again, my guts were hurting so bad I could barely swallow the sausages and mash she'd cooked up specially.

At half past eight I forced myself to go home to Jacko's, feeling sure Pete must've gone by then. That maybe it'd never happened, that I'd imagined it all. Or that, at the very worst, Jacko had flipped from too much acid and would've come to his senses and feel sick at what he'd done. Come to me and say how sorry he was.

When I got back Jacko was sitting on the couch by himself, watching the footy, like normal.

I breathed a sigh of relief. 'So he's gone then?'

'Who? Oh Pete. Nah, he's in bed. I just wanted to watch this first. Want a beer?'

'You mean he's still here? In your bed?'

'Yep.'

I swallowed hard. 'Jacko, do you know what you're doing mate? You're no poof. Are you?' My voice went all sort of stupid and squeaky at the end.

'What if I am? What's it to you, anyway?' he said, handing me a beer. 'Tell you what, it's the best fucking sex I've ever had. Heaps better than those loose sluts that hang round here. Or Beck the bloody virgin always sooking around over her pussy brother. Pete's something else.'

I had to force myself not to gag on the beer in my mouth. 'You're joking right? You're pulling some stunt to pay out on me, aren't you?' It had to be a joke.

'Never been more serious in my life. I tell you mate, he's totally cool. Last night was intense. Something happened man, something crazy.' He took a swig from his stubbie and shook his head with a smile like he was remembering something good.

'For fuck's sake, shut up! You're freaking me out. What the fuck? You're gay now is that it? All these years we've been best mates and really you've just wanted to get inside my daks?'

He laughed. 'Fuck no! Jesus, where'd you get that stupid idea? As if I'd go anywhere near your filthy pants.'

I got up from the couch and walked over to my bedroom. 'I can't take any more of this bullshit. I'm going to bed and when I wake up you're going to be Jacko again.' I slammed the door behind me. It was all I could do to stop from screaming.

'What's up with Brian?' I heard Pete ask from the bedroom.

I smoked cigarettes till my pack was empty, then wanked myself sore staring at tits and pussy, till I finally fell asleep.

I hoped it'd all be over in a day or two; that the acid would wear off and Jacko would go back to being his usual self. But every night I came home from the servo to find him and Pete snuggled up on the couch like Siamese twins. I couldn't hack it, banged my door and didn't come out of my room till I heard them go to bed. Then I'd come out and turn the telly up really loud so I wouldn't have to listen to Pete's laughter and Jacko's moans.

It got so I could hardly bear to look at Jacko, especially after he started wearing makeup, outlining his eyes in black. Some of the young fellas started copying him, thinking they were cool. But I didn't. I missed the old Jacko. My best mate had disappeared, swallowed whole by some guy in a puffy shirt.

After a couple of weeks of their carry on, I stayed away from the house altogether. Jacko was no fun anymore, all he wanted to talk about was Pete. I couldn't take it. I slept back at Mum's some nights, till she drove me mad, then over at Steve's. But he was going strange on me too. He'd gone to some freaky church and was carrying on about how he'd been saved. Kept trying to get me to go with him. Life was shitty.

One afternoon, when I went back to the house to pick up some more of my stuff, it was just Jacko sitting on the couch. No Pete.

'He's gone,' he said, smearing black eye-shadow all over his face with the back of his sleeve. 'Gone to Sydney.'

'Oh,' I said, but inside I was giving three loud cheers. 'Oh well. Maybe things can get back to normal now.'

'He said he doesn't want me to come. What's gone wrong, man?' He leaned over onto my shoulder, his chest shuddering.

I patted him on the back of his sweaty t-shirt. 'Don't worry about it mate. You've still got me. You'll be right. Let's go get a bottle of something hey? To, um... help you, you know, forget.' Finally it had ended. I'd have my best mate back. I was going to celebrate.

'I won't forget. Why's he doing this? I don't get it. What's his problem?'

I had to turn my head away. I couldn't look at him like this anymore. 'He's no good, man. I knew it from the start, but you were so...'

'No mate, you've got it wrong. He's everything. I'm never going to get over this.'

'Shit, what sort of talk is that? Look me in the eye,' I grabbed his chin like he was a kid and forced him to look at me. 'Repeat after me, "I'm going to be alright."'

'I'm going to be alright.'

'There, you see. Everything's going to be fine. Let's go get that bottle and forget about it. I'm always here for you, you know that.'

He dragged his sleeve across his face to wipe off the snot. 'You're right mate. Thanks.'

So we drove up the pub and bought a couple of bottles. Steve came round with another bag of dope and we all had a great time. Just like the old days. We got Jacko to wash the shit off from around his eyes and tried to make him laugh. A couple of times it seemed like the old Jacko had come back.

Steve went home and I staggered to bed, leaving Jacko with the bottle and the bag, staring at some crappy late night movie. He seemed like he was going to be fine. I was looking forward to having my mate back, to going back to being the terrible two, just us mates. No one in between.

It was me that found him in the morning, sprawled out on the cement under the house in a puddle of his own spew. His lips blue. I saw the crushed packet of Winfield's and the empty bottle of sleeping pills. I saw the note with Pete's name on the front.

I rolled Jacko onto his back and put my mouth over his. Breathed into him, like I'd done before with Douggie, till he coughed and moaned and vomited some more. And then I called the ambulance.

After I'd helped wheel him out to the road and slid him into the back of the van, I didn't stay to watch as they drove away. I didn't go to the hospital. I went back under the house and found that note. The one to Pete.

It was full of words of love and broken hearts. Tear stained.

I burnt it.

Closed Ward

Brian

'I've had it,' I say to Douggie, but he doesn't answer. Don't know if he can.

I've come by myself to visit him today, borrowed the car from Mum. I'm back living at home for a while. Trying to sort shit out. Jacko's rung a couple of times since I left his place, pretending nothing's changed, and maybe it hasn't for him but it sure has for me. I can't do it anymore. He's still tripping every weekend and rooting anything that moves, boys and girls, but I don't want any part of it. I've had enough of his bullshit. Always being treated as if I didn't count.

Douggie's enough to worry about, without Jacko as well. My shoulders are only so big.

'Doug? Can you hear me?'

He's sitting in a plastic chair with a blanket wrapped around his shoulders like a cape. The old Douggie would've been racing around the room pretending to be a superhero. This one can't even focus his eyes long enough to tell who I am. His chin keeps nodding down to his chest, then he twitches. They must have him on super strong meds. Mum said they were trying something new after he tried to escape again the other night. Kind of proud of him for that.

I sit beside him staring out the window at the hospital car park, edged by some crappy dried-out gardens. Crows call to each other on a straggly gum tree.

'Wha...?' He turns and sees me at last. I've been here ten minutes. 'Bri?'

'Yep, it's me Douggie. How's it hangin'?'

Head wobbling on his neck like a doll that's lost too much stuffing, he purses his lips and swallows hard. 'Been better.'

'Need a drink, mate?'

He nods so I go over to the water dispenser. I have to step over a woman who's lying flat on her stomach in front of it, making soft bubbling noises. This place is totally freaky. And it stinks. Even though they're not allowed to smoke in here anymore the reek of twenty years-worth of chain smoking oozes from the walls.

It's the closed ward. Like a prison for loons. I have to fill in a form a mile long every time I visit and then be frisked and buzzed through the bullet-proof door that slides open once the guard is in place.

The water I pour into the paper cup is freezing and the air-conditioning is up way too high. No wonder Douggie's got a blanket. I step over the woman and head back to Douggie but I spill most of it when a jabbering old man grabs my elbow. A nurse comes and takes him away. I keep my eyes fixed right on Douggie so I don't have to see the other crazies. There are too many. Some stand swaying from side to side, others watch the midday movie, others sit like Douggie in front of the window. Probably haven't moved since the nurses put them there in the morning.

'Here you are.' I hand it to him and he takes a grateful sip.

'So, yeah. Like I was saying. I've had it with Jacko and all his shit. I just don't give a fuck.'

Douggie takes another sip and stares back out the window.

'Mum's coming tomorrow. She's doing better now, hey? Don't you think? Not drinking so much anyway. Trying to cut down myself. Though shit, it's boring. What're you supposed to do if you don't get wasted?'

Douggie wobbles his head back in my direction and looks at me with his eyes half-crossed.

'Saw Beck the other day. Dyed her hair blonde now, looks pretty cool. Not so wasted and Emo like before. She says hi.'

He moves his lips but nothing comes out. He tries again. 'Beck?'

'Yeah. She says hi.'

'Beck.' He smiles through the dirty glass as a station wagon pulls in across the bitumen.

'Don't know if she's going with anyone. Maybe I should go round and see her, invite her over to watch some footy or something. Reckon she'd like that?'

He rolls his eyes and mumbles something that sounds like 'hopeless.'

'So what do you think? I'm looking fit or what?' I stand up and pat at my belly which only jiggles half as much as it used to. 'Been doing pushups and shit. I'm up to fifty.'

He's back staring out the window at the crap view like he's forgotten I'm there. I wait a few minutes then say, 'Reckon I might go then. Mum probably needs the car for shopping. Anyway, congrats about the appeal, you'll be out of here in no time.' Well, at least not a lifetime. Lucky he didn't kill the old bird.

He's still staring.

I put my hand on his shoulder and speak closer to his ear. 'I'm going now.'

'Brian?' he says like he's only just realised I'm there. 'Bri?'

Then he wraps me into a massive bear hug so tight I can hardly breathe.

'You're right, Douggie, you're right.' I try to peel his arms from me but he won't let go. He's clinging to me like I held onto that log that day in the creek. Hanging on as if I can save his life.

But I can't. I've only ever had enough strength to keep my own head above water.

'Got to go, Douggie. See you next time, hey?' I pat his back till his grip weakens and I can slide out between his elbows. 'Be good. Don't do anything I wouldn't do.'

My attempt at a joke doesn't seem funny even to me. I back away, babbling on and on about how Mum really needs to do some shopping, making worse jokes till I'm at the door pressing on the buzzer, signalling for the guard to get the bloody door. Quick. I don't even flick a glance behind me as I edge sideways through the gap as it slides open.

Back at the car I rev the engine till it screams and reverse out of the car park with a screechy, crash over the speed-bumps and roar out onto the road. With my foot to the metal I drive and I drive until I can't see any more for fucking tears. I pull over and yell every swear word I know at God. For what he's done to my little brother.

And me.

Meat Tray

Beck

'Number forty-seven. Number forty-seven,' yells an old guy in shorts and a singlet, a tray of meat in his bulky arms.

I've been sitting here in the crowded beer garden of the pub closest to Uni for over an hour. It's late Brisbane summer, stinking hot and sweaty. My legs are glued to the plastic chair, pools of sweat under my knees.

I'm waiting for Pete. He's up from Sydney, and though we've barely spoken since he decided it was better to fuck Jacko than be friends with me, he says he wants to make up, that Jacko was a mistake. I knew that already.

'Last call. Number forty-seven.'

All around the pub, hands fumble in pockets and purses as people pull everything out looking for the lucky ticket. I crane my head searching for the winner.

'Here! That's me! Forty-bloody-seven!'

In the far corner near the dunnies, a fella about my own age with slicked-back brown hair, bad skin and heavy eyeliner leaps from his chair, waving a crumpled pink ticket. As he pushes his way through the drinkers his face becomes horribly familiar. Bloody Douggie.

'Here mate, here! I'm the lucky winner!'

Two steps away from the tinfoil tray loaded with chops and steaks and mounds of sausages, he trips and falls into my lap. I push him off and everyone laughs.

'Fuck you guys!' he shouts, struggling to his feet. 'I'm the winner!' He shoves his crumpled ticket into the raffle man's hand. I don't think he even realises it's me. He must be having one of his bad days.

'Yep. Number forty-seven all right. It's your lucky day. She's all yours. Don't eat her all at once.' The man passes over the tray. Droplets of watery blood fall onto the brick pavers.

'Shit, it's heavy.'

'Ten kilos of top quality meat there, son – better get it home and into the freezer.'

'You kidding? I've got to celebrate. I've never won a bloody thing before.'

He looks around like he's going to give a speech but everyone's already lost interest and turned back to each other and their beers. I sort of smile up at him. I'm glad he won; he deserves a break or two.

'Hey you guys, I'm the winner. Me, Doug Spencer, star in the making. On my way up you know, all the way to the top. This is just the beginning. Cool! Who wants a drink on me?'

That gets their attention.

'Are you for real?'

'Free beer?'

'The beer's on you is it mate?'

'Good on ya.'

Douggie stands clutching his meat tray, ecstatic, the centre of attention, his eyes darting from the cool guys he wants to impress to all the girls he's probably dreaming of screwing.

'Yeah sure,' he says. 'Free beer for everyone!'

A roar goes up and the bar is almost knocked over in the rush.

'You sure you've got the money for that son?' The old bloke taps him on the shoulder.

'Course I've got the money,' Douggie hisses, pulling a handful of orange twenty-dollar bills from his jeans pocket. 'Got my pension cheque today.' He holds the money high. 'The beer's on me!'

Shirtless, shoeless students bump past my table in the stampede to the bar, pressing into each other, four deep at the counter, waving their arms and shouting orders.

Douggie throws himself into the chair next to me, plonking the meat tray onto the table and lighting a cigarette.

'Meet a winner,' he says, smiling his best movie star grin. 'Douglas Spencer, prize winner and star on the rise, at your service.'

'Yeah right, Douggie,' I say. 'Since when are you a star on the rise?'

'Know me from the telly do you?'

'Douggie,' I sigh. 'It's me, Beck. Where's Brian? Does he know you're out?'

'Fuck Brian. Anyway, what's it to you?'

'It's me, Rebecca Roche, Becky. Remember? Russ's sister? Primary school? All those parties at Jacko's? Got me now?'

'Oh yeah, Beck. You look different. Didn't recognise you with your hair blonde. Anyway, want a drink? Want to get it on with a winner?' He puts his hand on my knee. 'It'll be the best you ever had.'

I lift his fingers off one by one. 'Hands to yourself, Douggie. I'll have a drink though, scotch and dry please.'

'Sure, sure.' He races over to the bar where the queue parts to let him through. 'Got your beers everyone?'

'They got 'em all right,' says the barman. 'Now you'd better cough up. That's seventy-three bucks, mate.'

Even from here I see Douggie's eyes bulging. 'What?'

'Do the words "the drinks are on me" remind you of anything?'

'Yeah, but shit. Seventy-three dollars?'

'There's a lot of punters here on a Thursday.'

Douggie pulls four twenty-dollar bills from his pocket and hands them over. 'That's it, but. No more free beer. The rest of my money's in a Swiss bank account.'

'Yeah right mate, whatever you say.'

Doug buys my scotch and a bourbon for himself and weaves his way back to the table.

'Thanks,' I say, taking a swig. 'I needed that.'

'I'm feeling great,' says Douggie. 'Deadset unreal, top of the world. I'm a fucken star!' he shouts, standing up and waving his arms.

'Sit down, Douggie. Everyone's looking.'

'So what's new, they're always looking. Price you pay for being famous.' He sits back down and puts his hand on my boob. 'You've got great tits.'

I slap him away with a laugh. 'Behave yourself or I'll call Brian to come get you. Anyway, I thought you were still in lock-up, I mean, hospital. How come you're out?'

'Shit. Why'd you have to go and say that? I was feeling so good. Forgot all about that bloody hole. Hey, I know. Let's have some music. I feel like dancing. You like dancing?'

Downing his bourbon, he fights his way to the jukebox and grins as he punches in letters and numbers. He stops at the bar on the way back and gets some more drinks.

'Why are you all by yourself anyway?' he asks. 'Where's Jacko and them?'

I don't answer, deliberately concentrating on lighting my cigarette.

'Hey, hey. What do you know? Jacko's had the boot. Things are looking up. I won the prize. I got the girl. I've got an appointment with an agent first thing in the morning.'

'What sort of an agent? The FBI?' Best to humour him I reckon.

'Music, man, music. I've been playing the guitar, written some songs. Top ten I'm telling you. I'm a bloody star.'

A Billy Joel song starts up on the jukebox.

'My song,' says Douggie.

'Urgh, Billy Joel, that old fart. He gives me the creeps. What's that doing on the jukebox?'

Douggie sings along, some stupid lyrics about how even though he's crazy he might just be the one I'm looking for. 'Come on. Sing with me. Or do you want to hear my latest song. One I wrote? Yeah. Let's go down the river and I'll sing it just for you. A concert for one.'

Have to get out of that one fast. 'Um. Thanks but no thanks, Douggie. Actually, I'm waiting for Pete.'

'What? That poofter? When you could have a piece of this arse.' He stands up and wiggles his bum in my face. 'What do you reckon? Good arse or what?'

I laugh. 'Not bad. A bit pointy.'

'What do you mean pointy?' He twists his head around trying to get a look. 'It's not pointy. It's perfect. Plenty of people would kill for an arse like this.'

'Yeah right. It's perfect. Can I have another drink?' The first couple of scotches haven't numbed me like I'd hoped. I need more alcohol to help wrap the steel tighter around me before facing Pete.

'Sure. I'll be right back. Same again?'

I stare at the meat tray while he goes to the bar. A pool of blood stained water is spreading out under the foil onto the table and the smell of butcher is wafting through the double layer of cling wrap.

Douggie splashes my drink down in front of me. 'Here you go.'

'Do you ever feel like that, Douggie?'

'Like what?'

'Like a meat tray?'

'What the fuck are you talking about?'

'You know. Like you're nothing but a pile of raw meat with only a bit of plastic holding you together.'

'Are you stoned or what?'

'Forget it.'

'Yeah, snap out of it. They reckon I'm crazy. You're bloody weird. Anyway, we're having a great time, aren't we? This place is raging and I'm flying man. Unreal! The stuff the doc's got me on really kicks in when I get pissed.'

'Shit, maybe you shouldn't be drinking. It could be dangerous.'

'What? Like I might go crazy?'

'I didn't mean it like that.'

'Don't freak out on me. I'm cool. Everything's great'

A Justin Timberlake song blasts out of the jukebox speakers.

'That's mine too,' he yells. 'Check this out.' And he jumps up onto his chair and starts doing dance moves from the film clip, pointing and gyrating.

All around the beer garden people look up to watch the show and laugh.

'Hey look. It's J.T.'

'Sit down, ya dickhead.'

I tug on the cuffs of his jeans. 'Come on, Douggie. Get down.'

Then I see something that stops the breath in my chest. 'Oh fuck.'

Across the garden, coming down the ramp from the train station is a gang of long-hairs, and in the middle of the group is a boy with dirty hair, torn jeans, and a leather jacket even though it's way too hot for one. Jacko.

'Sit down. For God's sake, don't let him see me.'

'Who?' Douggie asks, clambering down and craning his neck.

'Don't look. It's Jacko.'

'You want me to sort him out for you?'

I keep my head down but can't help smiling. 'Thanks, but it's okay. I just don't want him to see me.'

I can't stop staring though, sneaking my head around Douggie to catch glimpses of Jacko through the crowd. His eyes are bloodshot and at the back of his head his hair is matted into clumpy dreadlocks.

I cringe as he sidles up to a girl and slips his arm around her waist.

'That's it. I've got to go. If Pete turns up can you tell him I had to go home?' He and Jacko can have a lovely reunion for all I care. I stand up, sculling the last of my drink.

'Don't go yet. Come on, stay and party with a winner. How about another scotch? Forget about that loser. We can make him jealous if you like.'

'Thanks.' I smile and muss his hair. 'But I've got to go.'

'Beck! Rebecca!' Jacko's voice tears through the din of the pub. He knocks people out of the way to get to me. I turn my back, close my eyes and hold my breath but it doesn't make him go away.

He grabs me from behind and spins me around.

'Hey, mate, let her go,' says Douggie. 'She doesn't want to see you.'

'What's it to you? Fuck! Douggie? When'd they let you out of the loony bin? Thought you were locked up for life.'

Douggie shrugs.

Jacko's fingers are digging into my arms. 'What's going on? Where's Pete? Why doesn't he answer my calls? He's here, isn't he?'

I press my lips tight together and focus on the meat tray. Fuck him.

He shakes me. 'Look at me. Tell him I've got to see him. I miss him something fierce. Where is he? Tell me for fuck's sake.'

'Nine chops, sixteen sausages, five T-bone steaks,' I mutter under my breath.

Jacko's face is purple, spit flies as he yells, 'Fucken stop it! I love him. I fucken love him. Understand? I've got to see him.

I've just got to.' The beer garden crowd grows quiet, suddenly interested.

'Hey, leave her alone!' Douggie tries to pull Jacko away but is backhanded into a chip-bark garden bed for his trouble.

'Come on Beck. Tell me where he is and I'll go. That'll be the end of it. Tell me!' He jerks me so hard my head rattles.

'Eight rashers of bacon, twelve spare ribs.'

'Stop it. Fucken stop it. I'm sorry, all right? Is that what you want? I'm fucken sorry. Sorry I ever fucked you and that's for sure.'

Tears form in the corners of my eyes but I lift my face to his and show him that he no longer exists. 'Leave. Me. Alone.'

Douggie hurtles across the pub, flying at Jacko with all the strength of drunken fury. He flings himself at Jacko's waist and tackles him onto the table, squashing the meat tray. Glass shatters on the floor.

'Fuck off, Douggie.'

Douggie jabs knotty fists into Jacko's sides as he flounders on top of him on the table. Jacko wraps him up and rolls them both off, falling with the tray of meat to the ground. The plastic wrap bursts open and pieces of bloody meat and coils of sausages tumble like entrails onto the bricks. Douggie untangles himself, gets up, does a karate yowl and runs at Jacko, kicking him in the chest.

'That's it,' Jacko grunts, taking off his jacket. 'Now you're going to get it, you mad bastard.' He takes his first proper swing at Douggie and splits his lip. It starts to bleed.

'My face!' Douggie squeals, putting his hand to his mouth.

Jacko throws another punch and catches him on the ear, hard.

'Stop it, Jacko!' I scream. 'Leave him alone!'

'Fuck him. Fuck the loony!'

Jacko hits him again and again so I jump onto his back and lay into his head.

A circle forms around us and the chant, 'Fight! Fight!' goes up. Douggie gets in one good kick to Jacko's balls that doubles him over and hurls me to the ground. Jacko struggles up, furious. He smashes his fist into Douggie's face and sends him crashing into the garden.

'Help him!' I yell. 'For God's sake! Someone!'

Through the crowd I see a large shape approaching. A thickset young man in greasy overalls forces his way through the circle. Brian. He grabs Jacko, lifts him till his feet are dangling, then throws him face first into the crowd.

'Get the fuck away from my brother, you cunt!'

Jacko staggers to his feet. 'Brian! I ... Um ... He started it. Fucken attacked me for nothing.'

Brian shoves a giant fist under his nose but then thinks better of it, and lets him go. Jacko topples backwards, mashing the last of the sausages into the bricks.

Brian bends down over Douggie, closes his arms around him and hoists him upright.

'You right mate? Everyone's been looking for you. Thought I might find you here.'

'Hey, Bri,' says Douggie through thick lips and blood. 'I won the meat tray.'

CHAPTER 16
Thrill Seekers
Brian

Muddy spray hits my lips as the boat thumps over small waves, heading east along the river. Ray, the head mechanic at work, is taking me and Bruce, the other apprentice, fishing for the day because we did so well on our tech exam.

Ray's not a bad bloke, for an old fella I mean. Even though he must be at least forty he still swears and stuff and lets us have the radio playing in the workshop, doesn't mind if we muck around a bit as long as the work gets done. Didn't think his boat would be this fancy though. It's three thousand times better than Dad's dinghy was, that's for sure. This is a proper cruiser. It's got a cabin and a huge fucking motor that roars like a Harley. Cool.

Bruce is hanging over the edge looking green, clutching his guts, but I'm loving it. Especially now we've left the river and the stink that hangs in the mangroves. The sky stretches blue and clean above our heads.

Reckon Douggie would have a ball out here. Pity I had to take him back to the loony bin yesterday. But I had to. He was okay about it, stuck out his puny chest and went in. Even though he's stuck in that shitty hole he doesn't let it get to him. He makes a break for it whenever he can, runs wild for a few days till they lock him back up. That takes a lot of guts. He even took on Jacko that day in the pub. He's the bravest kid I know, my little brother.

I stare at the water, watching as it slowly changes from brown to blue as we speed out into the bay. I think about me and Douggie and Steve and Beck and Russ, about how things went from fun to fucked faster than a summer storm hits.

I think about Jacko and me. I can't get that story about David and Goliath, the kid who killed a giant with one stone from his slingshot, out of my head. Reckon that's how I felt when I threw Jacko to the ground.

Funny thing is though, it was only when I picked him up and saw his feet dangling that I realised I was bigger than him. I've probably been head and shoulders taller for the last five years, just never noticed, still in awe of him and that bloody leather jacket. Following his orders as if he was still the captain of our crazy raft, putting up with all his crap, trying to be like him, to be his right hand man. Looking up to him.

And all the time I was bigger. Much bigger.

'So, where to fellas?' asks Ray. 'Want to stop around here at Fisherman Island or go on further to St. Helena, check out the ruins?'

Bruce doesn't say anything, he's too busy spewing.

'Well I reckon that's one vote for stopping as soon as we can. What about you, matey?'

I shrug. 'Don't care, wherever.'

'Nah mate, I need more than that. You want to go see the ruins or stop here? Your trip, you make the choice.'

'What do you reckon?'

'Up to you mate. They're both good.' He glances over at Bruce, who's standing up wiping his mouth. 'Bruce can hack it if you want to go further, can't ya Brucie?'

He nods.

'Let's go to St. Helena then. I've always wanted to see that old jail,' I say.

Ray powers up the motor and turns the wheel. 'St. Helena it is. That wasn't so hard was it?'

In a cove on the sheltered side of the island, where we can see the crumbling sandstone walls of the convict prison, we drop anchor and cast in our fishing lines. The first fish is mine, and it's not even a catfish or an eel like we used to catch in the creek. It's a bream, a beauty.

'That's a keeper,' says Ray with a grin. 'Chuck him in the bucket. We'll cook him up later for lunch.'

'Good on ya,' says Bruce, who's feeling heaps better since we stopped.

Ray catches the next one, then Bruce, then I reel in another one, but they're all smaller than that first whopper.

'Let's call it quits, hey?' says Ray. 'We've got heaps of tucker for now and even some to take home. Reckon your Mum would like that big one for tea, Brian?'

'Yeah.' It'd feel real good to give Mum something for once.

We putter round the cove a bit till we find some flats to drag the boat up on, though we still have to jump out into the water and the bottoms of our jeans get soaked. Bruce and I collect kindling and make a fire while Ray does the scaling and gutting, then we each spear a fish onto the end of a stick and roast it over the flames. Ray hands out colas from the esky and I don't even care that it's not beer.

I feel so goddam good, I'm scared something bad's about to happen. That Ray will realise he's made a mistake in taking us out, suddenly notice I'm fat and useless like Jacko always used to say, and leave me here on the island with the ghosts of the convicts.

But he doesn't.

After handing me his fish to cook, he limps back over to the esky to grab some lemon and the bread and butter.

'What's with your leg, Ray?' asks Bruce.

I shoot him a look. You don't ask stupid questions like that, what if it's something bad? I hate it when people ask about Dad or Douggie. The answers are too long and sad. They're my private stories, to try to make sense of when I'm alone. But Ray doesn't seem to mind. 'Accident. Wasn't much older than you fellas are now. I was a bit of a bloody moron. Totally pissed with my mates, stole a car and pranged into a tree. Almost killed my best mate. Fucked my leg for life.'

'Shit,' we say.

'Yep. My mate's okay now but I still feel real bad about it. Should never have happened.' Ray stops mid-smear of butter. 'But you know what? That accident was the best thing that's ever happened to me, besides the missus and kids I mean. I was real wild in those days, and it stopped me right in my tracks. In hospital for months myself, and then that whole year visiting

Harry, I had lots of time to think, sort myself out.' He passes over a piece of bread with his big grease-stained hand. 'If it weren't for that bloody accident I'd be in jail now I reckon. Or dead.' He shakes his head. 'Funny how life works out.'

The fish is cooked, white flesh flaking away from the bones, so we peel away the blackened skin and lay the meat on the fresh soft bread, squeeze on some lemon and tuck in. Best lunch I've ever had.

Later, after we've stuffed ourselves like Christmas, we pack up, smother the fire with sand and wade back out to the boat. I'm so full I lie down to rest on one of the bench seats, my arm covering my eyes as the swell rolls under me. Bruce finally seems to have found his sea legs so Ray lets him have a turn steering the boat.

As we enter the river and the water gets murkier, Ray calls me over.

'Your turn now, hey Bri?'

I sit up and rub my hands through my hair. 'What? Drive the boat? What if I crash it?'

'You'll be right mate. Come on. Give it a go.'

I take the wheel but I'm so nervous my knees feel like they're going to give.

'That's the way,' says Ray, standing behind me. 'Now just point the nose down the middle of the river and keep going. Piece of piss.' Then he goes and lies down on the bench and closes his eyes. 'Give us a yell when you see the Uni.'

'But ...'

'You'll be fine.' He says with a yawn. 'Just keep steering down the middle and you can't go wrong.'

At first I'm fucking petrified but after a while I realise it's really not that hard. Bruce lies down too and I stand like a crusty old seadog at the wheel of my ship, feet wide apart to keep my balance, my hands steady.

Looking down the river I steer a straight course, right down the middle like Ray said. Feeling ten feet tall with a chest as wide and strong as a bear's, I roll with the movement of the boat. Salty water sprays my face and my cheeks stretch into a mighty grin.

Suddenly it comes to me. A plan. A great one. I'm going to save up and buy myself one of these big boats, maybe even a bigger one with sails and beds and shit, so that by the time Douggie gets out for good we'll be set to go. We'll steer out of this bloody river like we should've done all those years ago on our raft, sail out into the bay and just keep going east. Far. All the way to Fiji or Hawaii, whatever we hit first.

We'll sail into the world, free and brave and ready for adventures, good and bad.

Ready at last to be what we were always meant to be, thrill seekers.

If you liked Thrill Seekers,
you might like other titles in the
Cutting Edge series.

The following is an extract from
another Cutting Edge title. It's the
first chapter of Ecstasy by
A. C. Flanagan

CHAPTER 1

I am just 17 and my life is over. Head spinning, hands shaking, I need to throw up again. The lights are so bright I can only squint. I can hear people passing, but they're just blurs.

Sitting here, sweat carving lines through my make-up, I feel as if everyone is judging me. The seats either side of me are empty. People are standing, rather than sit next to me – the junkie. Funny, isn't it, that I'm drowning in a sea of people, but if I died in front of them, it'd be alone.

I came here with Mai-Ling but they took her away, through those clear plastic swing doors. She was totally out of it. I thought she had just partied too hard when she fell on the footpath and started throwing up. But then blood started trickling from her ears and nose and I panicked. I got her here as fast as I could but it was hard, no one would help. I haven't seen her since and nobody's telling me what is happening.

You think I am self-pitying. You're thinking I'm another spoilt rich kid whose daddy gave her everything. Shit, they called the cops before they called my father!

The only time anyone comes near me is to question me again. They want to know everything but I can hardly think, let alone focus on what they are saying. I'm still too smashed to concentrate and they know it, but they keep hammering me. I don't care what they want to know, I just keep on back at them: "Is Mai-Ling OK? Is my friend alright?"

They act like they don't hear me.

On and on they go with the same fucking questions, "What did your friend take? What did she drink? When did she start losing consciousness?"

I keep saying to them, I've already told you everything – just leave me alone!

Fuck, I'm going to throw up again!

It's been half an hour since I spewed but my stomach won't settle. My father is still not here, even though I've called him like a million times. I have no one and I'm scared.

"Carrie Jones?" a voice startles me from behind. As I turn I am face to face with two cops. I can hear the whole waiting room exhale. The cavalry has arrived! Someone to take the druggie away.

"Carrie?"

They want me to talk to them but the room is spinning and I can only hold my head in my hands and nod.

"I am Constable Adams and this is Constable Cummings; we need to ask you about what happened tonight."

Taking my hands from my face, the neon lights burn. I see a woman who could only be three or four years older than I am. The realisation is starting to hit me that I'm in a shit-load of trouble and things have gone way too far. If the police are here then something really terrible must have happened to Mai-Ling. Or am I still tripping and this is not real. But it feels real – too real.

I swallow hard to stop the tears, "Is Mai-Ling . . .?"

The Constable's face is blank as she glances at her partner. It is as if they are talking in some kind of silent code to each other.

"Is she alright?"

Still no answer.

"Is she?" I am screaming now, I need to know! "For Christ's sake, will someone tell me what is happening with Mai-Ling?"

My words have poured themselves into my tears and I can hardly catch my breath. "She was just pinging, right? You know, she's just high. She'll be okay now that she's spewed, right?"

The female cop sits down next to me and looks me straight in the eye. She's freaking me out. My heart is racing and sweat is pouring down my face. My hair is dripping wet and I can't stop shaking. She is still just staring at me like she's searching for a way to break the terrible news to me.

She puts her hand on my shoulder. "Mai-Ling is still unconscious. This is very serious. We don't know yet . . ."

I feel like I have been hit in the guts. "What do you mean it's serious? She hardly took anything!"

The other cop stands and holds out his hand. "Let's go and sit down somewhere quieter, Carrie."

"Let me see Mai-Ling. You can make the doctors let me see her, I know you can."

"The best way to help Mai-Ling at the moment is to tell us everything that happened tonight."

"I've told them everything. I don't know anything else."

"I know but we need to ask you some more things."

"What things?"

"Come on, let's find a quieter place."

This guy is making out like he wants to help me but I don't trust him. My father has told me a lot about how the police get people to say things which get you into trouble. He's got a shit-load of stories about how they pretend to be your friend but really they're just trying to get you to say something bad. I don't trust them.

"I need my father to be here. He's a lawyer. I can't speak to you until he's here."

They stiffen the minute I say "lawyer". They're going to start pressuring me now, I can tell.

The woman cop is smiling at me with this fake I-care-about-you smile. "Carrie, Mai-Ling's mother is on her way. Don't you think she deserves to know what happened?"

"I already told the doctors what she took."

"You told them she had a tablet at a party. What was it?"

"I already told them."

"You need to tell us."

"Fuck! It was an ecstasy tablet. Okay?"

"Who did she get it from?"

"From this guy at the party. He had lots. Everyone was taking them. If there was something wrong we'd all be sick, right?"

The male cop keeps looking straight at me and asks his next question. "What's the name of the person who gave Mai-Ling the tablet?"

"I need to see my father! Where the *fuck* is my father?"

"I don't know where your father is, but Carrie, we need to know now. You want to help Mai-Ling, don't you?"

"Of course I fucking want to help Mai-Ling. She's my best friend! What do you think I am?"

"Did you take one of the tablets as well?"

"No."

"You took something though."

"What does that matter?"

The female cop stares at me again like she's my mother. Stupid bitch, she thinks she's so cool in her uniform and that shiny badge.

"I took a half, okay. I told Mai-Ling to only take a half. She hadn't taken it before and I told her to just take a half. But she didn't listen!"

"Can you tell us what happened from the beginning? From when you got to the party?"

"I need my father here first."

The woman cop looks over at her partner. He is shaking his head. I hear him whisper something like, "Go steady on her, she's just a kid." The woman cop is glaring back and I can't make out what she's saying. The guy cop sits down next to me.

"Look, I know this is hard for you. Your friend is really sick and you're feeling pretty sick yourself. We're not trying to make things harder for you."

"I need to call my father."

As I fumble for my mobile phone it starts to ring. "Dad?"

It's not him but his girlfriend, Anne.

"I need to speak to my dad."

She is telling me that he is out at the moment but she will get him to call me the minute he gets back.

"But I need him to come now . . ."

She has already hung up. She treats me like I'm nothing. Fuck! I'm in the hospital for Christ's sake and his girlfriend is screening his calls! I want to cry but I need to scream.

The woman cop is looking at me like she actually understands. "Come on, let's go to the Ladies and you can wash your face."

The mention of water reminds me how thirsty I am. Now, I cannot think of anything else.

"I need water."

She brings me a plastic cup. I scull it and am desperate for more. She brings me one cup after another. It's like I'm a bloody camel.

I'm still drinking when a woman runs into the waiting room screaming Mai-Ling's name. She stops dead, looks at me and my whole stomach knots. It is Mai-Ling's mum and she looks like a train wreck, clothes thrown over pyjamas. Jesus, she is walking over to me, face screwed up. She has no idea.

"Carrie, Carrie, where's my Mai-Ling? What's happened to her?"

She is so unaware, she has no fucking clue.

"I don't know, Mrs Truong. She's in with the doctors I think."

She looks at the two cops and then back at me. "Carrie, what's going on?"

The policewoman saves me from answering. She moves Mai-Ling's mum away and starts talking to her. God, I feel like crap. She is crying and clutching at the policewoman guiding her over to one of the nurses. The other cop is still sitting with me. He is watching Mai-Ling's mother too and I know what he is thinking. How glad he is that it's not him having to tell her; how thankful he is that he is the one left here with me. He is like my father, unemotional when it comes to real life. He catches me looking at him and makes an oh-shit kind of face. I make the same and decide that my father can do what he does best, arrive in time to clean up the mess.

"My dad's not coming. What do you want me to tell you?"

We wait in a small office to the side of the waiting room. I see Mai-Ling's mum through the glass, sitting in the waiting room crying. Others are watching her but no-one goes to see if she's alright. I should be with her but instead I am here telling two strangers how her daughter came to be passed out in the emergency unit of the Royal Prince Alfred Hospital.

The policewoman leans towards me. "We need to know exactly what happened tonight. From the beginning."

"There isn't much to tell. It was just some stupid party with a bunch of stupid people getting drunk and off their faces."

"Can you tell me where this party was? The address?"

"Somewhere in Newtown, near the train station."

The other cop chimes in. "Carrie we need you to be more exact."

"That's all I know. We went there with these guys we met in the city."

The policewoman asks, "Did you know these people?"

"No, not really, we met them at a nightclub earlier on. They said they were going to this party and said we could come."

"How old are you, Carrie?"

"Seventeen."

"And Mai-Ling?"

"Seventeen."

I can tell she is thinking that I'm trash. I have a private education, go to one of the best private schools in Sydney, but I'm still trash. None the less she is keeping up her I-really-care-about-you tone.

"Okay, what happened when you got to the party?"

"We had a couple of drinks and kind of hung around a bit."

"Were you with Mai-Ling?"

"Sort of, she was talking to this cute guy so I hung back."

"What were you drinking?"

"Bundy and Coke."

"Did you mix your drinks yourself or did someone give them to you?"

"The guy Mai-Ling was talking to got them for us."

She looks over to her partner with a knowing look. As she turns back, her eyes flick to the glass wall behind me. I spin around to see what she's looking at. It's Mai-Ling's mother. As the doctor speaks to her, her sobs become a wail. They take her by the arm and help her up. I try to run out there but the woman cop grabs my arm. Her partner gets up and leaves the room. Mai-Ling's mother is being taken through the plastic doors into the emergency ward.

"I have to go with her. Let me go with her!" My whole body is shaking. I know something bad has happened, something really bad.

"You need to stay here." The constable insists.

"She's my friend. She needs me."

"She needs her mother."

The reality hits. I am just the friend. Even though I'm the one who knows Mai-Ling better than anyone. Even though we shared all our thoughts and secrets, and were there for each other no matter what.

When push comes to shove, I'm not blood, so I'm nothing.

Mai-Ling did need her mother. She needed her more than most but she wasn't like girls our age. While we were all growing up in our flash houses on Sydney's North Shore, she was in Vietnam scraping together money to afford to go to school. I remember when she told me how she came to Australia in a boat no bigger than my father's yacht. Over 20 people including Mai-Ling and her folks crowded together for weeks until they got to Australia. Three people died on the way — one of them was her father. They had to throw his body overboard. If that wasn't enough, when they got here they were thrown into the detention centre at Villawood for three years until, finally, they got a visa and could stay. Her mother has worked 24/7 ever since to give Mai-Ling everything she never had herself. So, yeah, Mai-Ling needed her mum but she had me instead, and that's just life, isn't it?

My head has stopped spinning and now fear runs through my whole body in the place of the pain. The male cop walks back into the room and flashes his partner a strange look. I stand up and push the woman cop's hand off my arm. "I'm going to see Mai-Ling. We're done here!"

I start towards the door, but the constable's stern tone stops me dead. "We will have to do a drug test. You're not leaving until that is done."

I turn back. "You didn't tell me that before. Is that a threat?"

She shakes her head. "We need to make sure you're not at risk."

"Of what?"

"Some serious reaction. Like Mai-Ling's"

"But I'm fine!"

"It's the law."

"What law?"

The guy is shaking his head again and she is giving him a really dirty look. I suddenly get that they can't make me do anything, and she is just pushing me around because she feels like it.

"There's no law. I'm under-age so you'd have to get my father to okay it first, wouldn't you?"

The fog is lifting and I'm starting to think straight. Suddenly I'm wondering why the fuck I'm talking to these two anyway. What possible help is any of this to Mai-Ling? They know what she took, where she took it and the rest is just bullshit. I reckon the guy cop is thinking exactly the same, and it's this stupid bitch who has been watching way too much *CSI* and thinks she's some kind of *who knows what* that's keeping me here.

"So, are you arresting me or something?"

She keeps it up. "No, not at this stage but we do need a blood sample before you go."

I am getting out of my seat now and no-one is stopping me. "In that case, I'm leaving. You want a blood sample? You can wait until my dad gets here and ask him."

As I storm out, I can feel the tension between the two of them. I glance back and they have already started at each other.

Back in the waiting room, suddenly I'm sweating again. The water I drank before has helped but now I am feeling worse than ever. My head is aching and I need to sit down. My legs go to jelly as I reach for a seat. Shit, everything's gone black . . .

I am sitting in one of the plastic chairs but I don't remember how I got here. One of the nurses is taking my blood pressure. She smiles at me as she takes the monitor off my arm.

"Am I alright?"

"It's perfect. You can sit here as long as you need to."

As she stands up I grab her arm, "Mai-Ling, my friend, I came here with her. I need to see her."

She looks at me like she is trying to put a face to a name, "Is she a young Vietnamese girl?"

At last, someone who can tell me what is going on.

"Yes! Can I see her? Is she going to be alright?"

Her face says it all. "Sorry but you'll have to talk to the doctor about that."

"Which doctor? Where can I find the doctor?"

"Your friend is very sick. The doctors are still with her."

"But she'll be okay, right?"

Christ, the look on the nurse's face is horrible. It totally throws me and I start to panic.

"Right?"

I am insisting that she talks to me but she just stares back at me with a prepare-yourself-for-the-worst face. Or worse, that you-have-no-idea-how-serious-this-is face. Oh God, I want to wipe that look right off her face.

"RIGHT?"

I am pleading with her now. I need her to tell me that it is all going to be fine, but she's just staring at me. Tears are streaming down my face as I fumble for the words that I don't want to say.

"She's not going to die, is she?" They tumble out of my mouth anyway. "Is she?" I keep staring at her, "Is she?" Her hand's on my shoulder and she's shaking her head. Jesus!

Slowly, she says, "No-one knows yet. Your friend is still unconscious. The doctor will let you know if there is any change."

She takes her hand off my shoulder and leaves me sobbing. I can feel the eyes of the whole waiting room on me. Oh God, this can't be happening, there has to be a mistake, there has to be . . .

Life at the CUTTING EDGE
For more gritty reads in the same series

A Forgotten Tomorrow
TERESA SCHAEFFER
Savannah is alone, and haunted by painful memories. Can she learn to accept the things she cannot change?

Bone Song
SHERRYL CLARK
Melissa is running scared . . . and she daren't make friends or tell anyone her secret.

Breaking Dawn
DONNA SHELTON
Is friendship forever? Secrets, betrayal, remorse and suicide.

Don't Even Think It
HELEN ORME
One family's terrible secret.

Ecstasy
A C FLANAGAN
Carrie's supposedly dutiful friend, Mae-Ling, is fighting for her life after an ecstasy overdose. But Mae-Ling is not the only one hiding dark secrets.

Gun Dog
PETER LANCETT
Does having a gun make you someone? Does it make you strong or does it actually make you weak? Stevie is about to find out.

Hanging in the Mist
PETER LANCETT
Living in a high-rise crumbling tower block, with parents more interested in crack than you, is no fun.

Marty's Diary
FRANCES CROSS
How do you cope as a teenager when step-parents enter your life.

MindF**k
FANIE VILJOEN
Three disaffected youths, a beautiful hitch-hiker, a mind-blowing rock concert and a descent into darkness.

Seeing Red
PETER LANCETT
The pain and the pleasure of self-harm.

Ransom